To Micha

With best wishes on your 70th birthday

Henry J. Southern

The Phoenix Child

By

Henry J. Southern

Eloquent Books
New York, New York

Eloquent Books
An imprint of AEG Publishing Group
845 Third Avenue, 6th Floor - 6016
New York, NY 10022
www.eloquentbooks.com

ISBN: 978-1-60860-754-9

Printed in the United States of America

Book Design: Roger Hayes

Dedication

To Eileen

Kendal Berning in Oregon

And a little girl in Congleton, England

Acknowledgements

I am most grateful to the hard work and useful suggestions of my good friend and typist Sandra Hall. Also to Allan Fox, Rita and Dil Scrivens and all the rest of my friends and family who were so supportive at a very trying time.

Chapter 1

Jimmy

It was late summer, 1941, in the town of Shrimport; an important place, for it possessed both harbour and docks and occupied a prominent position on the south coast of England. The town's prominence had brought it to the attention of the Luftwaffe, and the German air force had subjected it to several heavy bombing raids during 1940–1941. Despite its battered appearance, the townsfolk continued to approach life with cheery optimism, both for their own and particularly for their children's sake.

Jimmy Atkins was an eleven-year-old who shared the townsfolk's optimistic mood despite the fact that he had already suffered harder than most. His mother had died when he was a baby and his father, a regular soldier, had moved into his mother's home, leaving Jimmy to be brought up by his widowed grandmother. Nothing had been heard of Jimmy's father since the British Army's retreat to Dunkirk in May 1940. Officially, Jimmy's dad was missing and presumed killed.

Jimmy's grandma was a kindly soul who had been a good substitute mother and, at eleven years old, he was regarded as a polite, caring boy who was very helpful and resourceful. In fact, life had made him mature for his age.

On this particular day, Jimmy had been sent to buy the weekly groceries at a store some distance from home. His grandma insisted on registering for their food rations at this store since Harry Hurst, the owner, had been sweet on her as a teenager. She was hoping that this former attraction would help her get anything extra that became available, over and above the normal food ration!

The journey had been uneventful. A few people were in the store and Jimmy had been served quickly. Now he had some free time before returning home to help his grandma get tea ready. Instead of following his normal route home and skirting Shrimport Municipal Park, he made his way to the play area for some fun. The decision was to prove both life-saving and have a major impact on his future.

Chapter 2

A Chance Encounter

As Jimmy approached the swings in the playground, he quickly assessed the situation. There were several young children with mothers fussing around them but, fortunately, there was an empty swing next to a boy who looked about Jimmy's own age and size. After carefully stowing his shopping bag, he mounted the swing and began to propel himself and, because of his open and pleasant nature, began to talk to his neighbour.

"Hello," he said, "my name's Jimmy. What's your name?"

"Hello Jimmy," was the reply, "my name's John Adams. It's great to have someone about my own age to play with."

"I'm eleven," replied Jimmy, "I start at the secondary school next month."

"I'm eleven as well," answered John, "but instead of going to secondary school I'm off to Canada with my mum. My Grandma Archer lives in Toronto and we are going to live with her. Dad's in the R.A.F. and he's already been posted to Canada to help at a flying training school that's been set up over there. I shouldn't really be telling you all this but I don't think you're a German spy and I can't see anyone lurking in the bushes. Isn't it great to be going to a country where you can ice skate and even ski all through the winter?"

"That's smashing," was the envious reply from Jimmy, "so you haven't bothered about getting a school place for September as you're leaving England?"

"Oh I do have a school place reserved for me in Shrimport," replied John, "while I was at my last school near R.A.F. Munby I passed the eleven-plus examination and had gained a free scholarship place at Lills Grammar School only a mile from where we were living. Seeing as we moved I got offered a place at Acres Hill Grammar School not far from our rooms, 'cos we didn't know how long we would be in Shrimport. My mum is going to write a letter to the headmaster telling him we are leaving the country."

"You don't live in a house at the moment then?" queried Jimmy.

"Well yes and no," was the reply. Up to a few days ago we did live in a house in married quarters adjacent to the airfield, but we left there quite recently to be nearby when we are called to board our ship. Now we've got this big room that's lounge, dining room, and kitchen with a little bathroom attached."

"Ooh you lucky things!" exclaimed Jimmy, "a proper bathroom and toilet. I've got to put up with a tin bath in front of the fire once a week, with my grandma fussing around and checking if my ears are clean. As for the lavatory, it's at the bottom of the yard. It ain't half cold in there in winter; you could freeze to the seat!"

"Are your parents in the forces?" enquired John.

"Me mum's been dead since I was a baby. I just can't remember her, and Dad's been missing since Dunkirk so me gran looks after me," replied Jimmy.

"That's real bad luck," sympathised John, "our rooms are a bit creepy though; they're over an empty car showroom that's boarded up. Mum says that it could be years before the building sees a new car again—that's if the bombs don't get it first. It's the only building that's standing for some distance after a bad bombing attack last winter. What property wasn't destroyed then was so badly damaged that the council pulled them down. There's still lots of scrap metals around and they plan to come back and sort them out. Otherwise it's really very, very quiet. Anyway, we'll be leaving in the next few hours as our ship sails on the morning tide. I can't wait!"

Just as he finished his explanation, a harassed lady came bustling up to the swings and, on seeing John, said, "Come on now, John, you'll have to say goodbye to your playmate. I've just come from the dockside and have been told that we have to board the ship straight away. They're sailing within the hour as there is a good possibility that the bombers will be back tonight."

"Aw Mum, just when I've found a place to enjoy myself and a friend to talk to," groaned John.

Mrs. Adams refused to be put off by her son's pleas and continued, "I've already packed the few things we are allowed to take and, worse still, I can't return the keys or pay the rent money to the letting agents as their property was destroyed in the last bombing raid. I've left the keys and money under a loose flagstone outside the door to the apartment and hope they'll have the good sense to look there. If not they probably have duplicate keys. Come on now, the taxi is waiting at the park gates; say goodbye and let's be off."

"It's a pity we've only just met. I'm sure we could have become good pals. Bye; Canada here I come," whooped John.

"Bye John, have fun," replied a slightly wistful Jimmy, thinking of the new life and great adventures his friend would be enjoying.

Jimmy sighed ruefully as he watched John and his mother disappear through the north gate of the park which led to the bomb-damaged suburbs of Elton where their rooms were situated. He continued to swing slowly, letting his thoughts wander on John's journey by sea and then on land to a home far from danger and with little in the way of food or clothing rationing.

How long he daydreamed he was not sure, but suddenly he came back to reality with a start. He was now on his own in the playground.

"Blimey, I'll be late for tea; Gran will think I've got lost!" he exclaimed. He sighed briefly, then picked up his canvas bag of groceries containing the basic rations for two persons for one week and left the now-deserted play area. He quickly made his way through the park, past the neat rows of cabbages and onions which now occupied the once-magnificent flower beds and reached the south gate. This exit led to the suburb of Milton where his grandma's modest terraced house was situated.

As he approached the gate, there came the dreaded noise of air raid warning sirens. Jimmy broke into a run, determined to get home before the bombs began to fall. He knew how worried his grandma would be if he was not with her at such a bad time.

Just as he left the park, an air raid warden suddenly appeared and grasped his arm, bringing him to an abrupt halt.

"Come on lad!" shouted the warden above the noise of the sirens, "there's going to be fireworks any minute now. Some bombers are coming in low over the sea. Luckily those Observer Corps chappies were up on the cliffs. They're the ones we've got to thank for raising the alarm."

The warden continued to hold onto Jimmy's arm as he was talking and quickly steered him into the depths of an underground air raid shelter on the perimeter of the park. The shelter was set amongst the trees and was approachable from all angles as the park's metal railings had been cut down some month's earlier to be melted down to help the war effort!

There were several people in the shelter already and Jimmy passed the next hour playing dominoes with some kindly old gentlemen under the light of a flickering paraffin lamp. When the dominoes palled he was also entertained with stories of the wars in the Sudan and South Africa in the 1890s and 1900s. His growing hunger pangs were eased by the gift of a corned beef sandwich and a mug of hot sweet coffee provided by these old soldiers who seemed prepared for all eventualities.

"It's more comfortable down here than in any trench!" one exclaimed.

At last the all-clear siren sounded and everyone filed out of the shelter hoping that their families, friends, and properties had been spared in the air raid. Darkness was falling as Jimmy hurried down the streets between the rows of terraced houses that, as he progressed, showed increasing effects of bomb damage. As he eventually reached the edge of the street where he lived, a terrible sight met his eyes.

Chapter 3

Disaster!

Jimmy's horrified gaze took in a scene of utter devastation that several properties in Smedley Street had suffered. A bomb had fallen in the centre of the road completely demolishing three houses on both sides and a fractured gas main had caused a huge fire to complete the destruction. The rest of the two rows of terraced houses had lost all their windows, front doors, and most of their roof slates.

A small crowd, held back by a couple of policemen holding a rope between them, had gathered at the end of the street intently watching the efforts of the fire brigade as they doused any lingering flames. The firemen had ignored the bomb-damaged water mains and brought in water from the special tanks constructed a few streets apart to provide the liquid for such emergencies. As Jimmy watched from the back of the group, he became aware that two of his near neighbours were talking about the air raid.

"They missed that big ship in the harbour but got us instead. What a relief almost everybody got to the air raid shelters," tutted Mrs. Jenkins.

"Aye, I think that Shrimport harbour and Milton got off lightly this time apart from poor old Granny Atkins and young Jimmy," murmured Mrs Smith, "they never left the house during air raids, but sheltered under the stairs. Unluckily for them they are the only casualties and there's no trace of them after this explosion and fire."

Jimmy stood there in total shock at these words, and then tears began to stream down his face as he realized that he would never see his dear, kind grandma again and, to make matters even worse, he was now totally orphaned. Slowly he gathered his wits and, realizing that no one in the watching group had recognized him in the gathering gloom, he quickly backed away into the darkness. He was totally aware that if he declared he was safe to his neighbours he would be quickly taken to the town hall and become the property of the local authority.

His reluctance to approach his neighbours had been triggered by recent English lessons at his former junior school where an over enthusiastic teacher had dwelt, at some length, on the life in the workhouse of the young Oliver Twist. No way could he contemplate spending the next few years in an institution and his young mind still imagined that places for the destitute and orphaned had not significantly changed in the hundred years since Charles Dickens had penned his novel on the life of the young lad.

Chapter 4

A New Hope

Jimmy shook his head, as though to clear it, as he stumbled away in the black-out from the shambles of his home in Smedley Street. What to do? Where to go? Most importantly, how to survive without the aid of adults, were all questions swirling around his brain as he walked along. Suddenly, he stopped, for he had reached the perimeter of Shrimport Park. The scudding clouds were now reflecting the glow of fires from the bombing raid and, in the distance, he could see the shape of the bandstand. He made his way to the structure which, whilst open to the elements for most of its 360 degrees, did possess a roof. He settled his young, grief-stricken body against one of the structures retaining posts and began to think.

The events of the past few hours had driven away the possibility of sleep for some time and Jimmy's agile young brain was put to the task of concentrating on his present predicament and his immediate future.

First of all, he had to find somewhere to live. The bandstand was fine for a balmy evening in late summer, but it could hardly be classed as being safe or secure and, once winter arrived, far from warm. Time dragged on with the youngster deep in thought then, suddenly—"Got it!" he exclaimed, speaking aloud to the wall as though it was a fellow conspirator, "John Adams and his mum have left their rooms to go to Canada and nobody in Shrimport knows them or that they've gone to another country. Since the estate agent's office has been bombed, nobody there is going to check up on them! Didn't she say that she had left the key under the flagstone? What a stroke of good luck."

Jimmy realized that if he wished to capitalize on this lucky break he had to move quickly, so he made his way slowly and carefully across the park and into the dark streets of Elton.

John Adams had been right about his accommodation. An earlier bombing raid had devastated part of the suburb and it was fairly easy to locate the showroom property as it was the only building still standing amongst the piles of rubble. The boarded-up windows had protected the building from the bomb blasts, so it had remained virtually intact with little damage to the roof as an added bonus.

Jimmy tentatively approached the rear entrance to the building and, as he neared the doorway leading to the upper rooms, a flagstone rocked slightly under his feet.

"Whoops," he gasped, "this must be where the keys and money are hidden." He quickly ran his fingers under the edge of the flagstone and was rewarded by finding two envelopes. One envelope contained a mortice key for the outer door and a Yale key for the apartment door. The second envelope contained four half-crowns (50p) and a short note addressed to the letting agent.

Quickly pocketing both note and money, Jimmy unlocked the outer door and entered the building. Carefully locking the door behind him, he switched on the light and made his way up the stairs.

Chapter 5

A Secure Roost!

Jimmy inserted the Yale key into the lock and pushed open the apartment door. The light from the landing revealed enough of the apartment for him to realize that with the wooden shuttering on the outside and heavy drawn curtains on the inside, the room's light would not be seen by any passer-by.

Satisfied that he was not going to break any black-out laws, he pressed down the light switch on the wall to the left of the open door. As light flooded the room Jimmy gasped in amazement for it was both stylish and well-furnished, a far cry from his grandma's frugal home.

Immediately to the left of the light switch was a box whose door was ajar. In the container was a gas meter with a slot for pennies and balanced on top of the unit were three of the copper coins. Alongside was the electricity meter; a far more up-to-date looking device operated by pushing shillings into its slot. Luckily, one of these silver coins glinted on the floor of the box containing the meter.

The whole of the floor was covered by a single carpet. "Blimey!" he exclaimed, "it must have taken a small army to carry this lot up the stairs!" To Jimmy, who winced each winter morning when he stepped out of bed onto bare linoleum, the floor covering was the height of luxury.

Jimmy's eye was then drawn to the room's furnishings.

In one corner were two neat little single beds, the sheets and blankets covered by smart, fairly new bedspreads.

Stepping further into the room, Jimmy's gaze then settled on a vast wardrobe and matching chest of drawers adjacent to the beds. Standing on the drawers was a large loud ticking alarm clock. Occupying the centre of the room was a small leather couch and, under one of the windows, stood a dining table surrounded by four chairs. Ranged along the far wall, adjacent to the closed bathroom door, was a two-ring gas cooker with a small oven underneath. Standing on one of the gas rings was a kettle. Next was a sink unit served by a cold water tap with a draining board on one side and a work surface on the other. The lower part of the unit was shelved and contained an arrangement of cleaning materials, pots, pans, and some tinned foods. This area was partially screened by a checked curtain which had been roughly pulled to one side. This completed the kitchen area.

Jimmy quickly walked across the room and cautiously opened the bathroom door a fraction, leaving just enough room to peer in. He was wise to do this for, although the bathroom had an opaque glass window covered by a lace curtain, it had not been properly blacked out. Jimmy took off his coat and hung it over the offending window before switching on the light. Oh joy of joys! There stood an actual indoor flush water closet, rather than the earth midden down a cold draughty yard. The said convenience having to be manually emptied, a not-to-be forgotten experience when the wind was blowing in the wrong direction. The room also contained a gas geyser with a flexible pipe that allowed hot water to flow either into the bath or adjacent wash basin.

As he went back into the main room, Jimmy suddenly realized how hungry he felt and he quickly emptied his bag of groceries onto the table. Finding a bread knife and cutting board on the kitchen work surface, he clumsily hacked a thick doorstep from the loaf he had purchased that afternoon. Very carefully he scraped a thin covering of butter from his meagre ration over the surface of the slice and tucked into the result along with an apple. Both items were washed down with a glass of tap water.

The alarm clock by the beds now showed it was well past ten o'clock. Jimmy carefully wound it up and, now feeling both physically and mentally exhausted after such a trying day, decided to turn in. He kicked off his shoes, padded to the door to switch the light off, and then groped his way back to one of the beds. Pulling a cover over him, he lay down on one of the beds and was soon fast asleep.

Chapter 6

Taking Stock

Jimmy awoke next morning to the sound of the ticking clock and, carefully carrying it over to one of the windows, he positioned it in a chink of light to read the time. Always an early riser, Jimmy observed it was a quarter-past six. He was tempted to return to bed for he still felt tired from the previous day's exertions but, realising there was so much to do, quickly carried out his ablutions in the bathroom. He thanked his lucky stars as that, in their haste to leave for the harbour, John and his mother had left behind towels, a tablet of soap, a half-used block of toothpaste in its tin and a well-worn toothbrush!

Returning to the dining table, Jimmy began to sort through the pile of groceries, along with the two ration books which had been his constant companions through most of the previous day's escapades. Pinned carefully to the back of one of the ration books was an official government circular addressed to all citizens giving details of each person's weekly food allowances along with an explanation of what clothing was rationed, as follows:

- Bacon and ham   4 oz.
- Sugar   8 oz.
- Butter   2 oz.
- Cooking Fats   8 oz.
- Meat (rationed by price) 1 shilling
- Tea   2 oz.
- Cheese   1 oz.
- Jam   2 oz.
- Plus 16 points per month for other rationed foods, subject to availability.
- Clothing coupon allowance 66 per person per year.
  - Examples: A three-piece suit 26 coupons
  - A woolen dress 11 coupons

Jimmy quickly realized he had the chance to obtain not only double rations but quadruple because John and Mrs. Adams' ration books were in evidence on one of the dining chairs! Getting enough food was not going to be a problem, but paying for it certainly was. The little purse sitting on the pile of groceries contained a total of six shillings and he was duty bound not to use the four half-crowns he had found. He determined to secrete the Adams' rent money just in case someone did turn up at the apartment!

Quick action was now called for and, after a hasty breakfast, Jimmy set about the task of earning some much-needed cash. He carefully observed if the coast was clear before locking the door. Then he took the precaution of hanging both door keys on a piece of string fastened around his neck and secreted it under his increasingly grubby shirt. Cautiously skirting the ruins surrounding his abode, he walked into the surrounding streets until he discovered a newsagent's shop. This premises, despite its windows being covered by boards to protect the meagre stock of sweets, cigarettes, and mineral waters such as lemonade and cream soda, proclaimed in bold white paint on a hastily tacked on plank *Business as usual— despite Mr. Hitler's recent calls*!

Jimmy entered the shop which was poorly lit by a small, bare light bulb and confronted the proprietor who, squinting and muttering to himself was consulting a list and noting down street names and numbers on the pile of newspapers in front of him. On seeing Jimmy, he reluctantly paused in his task and said quite tersely, "What do you want, lad? Can't you see I'm busy what with customers coming in and out all the time and me trying to mark up these papers? Goodness knows what time they'll get delivered."

"That's what I've come about," said Jimmy, "are there any jobs going as paper lads?"

"You're dead right there are," snorted Fred Jones, the proprietor, "what with the air raids and a lot of children being evacuated to country areas lads of your age are about as common as snowflakes in hell. When can you start?"

29

"Almost straight away," enthused Jimmy, "after I've helped you to mark up those newspapers."

"Good lad," chortled Fred, realising that life was going to get just a shade easier, "paper round pays sixpence a day and I'll give you another tanner if you come in earlier to mark up."

"Yes please," gasped Jimmy, hardly able to believe his good luck. He quickly did a mental calculation that he could count on a steady seven shillings per week for his efforts.

"Do you know if there is any place nearby looking for a lad to work on Saturday?"

"My, you are keen," chuckled Fred, "are things tight at home?"

"Yes," Jimmy swallowed hard as he answered for he launched into his first lie to protect his independence, "Dad's overseas somewhere and me mum isn't well and can't work much, that's why I didn't get evacuated as I was needed at home."

"Good lad," sympathised Fred, beginning to warm to this high-spirited youngster so anxious to earn for his family! "Aye, you've hit the nail on the head again, for Martin's grocers in the next street are looking for an errand lad. He'll snatch your hand off and probably pay you in cash and kind," he said with a knowing wink.

Jimmy quickly realized that *kind* meant the odd damaged tin, scrapings from a butter barrel, or a few links of mile sausages. The joke was a piece of meat every mile amongst the fat, breadcrumbs, and other unmentionables.

"A bag of mystery, that's the wartime sausage," he had heard his grandma declare.

"Come on then!" exclaimed Fred, breaking Jimmy from his reverie. "Get round this counter and start working or these newspapers will be history before they're delivered. I'm going into the back of the shop to make some tea and have a biscuit, want some?"

"Oh, yes, please," replied Jimmy, determined never to look a gift horse in the mouth.

"Just a minute!" exclaimed Fred, "here am I with a new employee and I haven't even asked what your name is. What do we call you?"

The realisation hit Jimmy like a punch in the stomach. There was no way he could use his real name for Jimmy Atkins was now officially a casualty of the war as he had perished in the last air raid! He remembered his goal; to keep out of the clutches of the town hall at all costs.

"John Adams," he blurted out, for he had suddenly realised that nobody would know about his brief friendship with a boy now well out into the Atlantic Ocean and heading for Canada.

"Right, John Adams. You're officially on the payroll now," Fred chuckled as he disappeared into the back room.

A relieved Fred, who was a widower, eventually returned with the tea and biscuits. Jimmy, after a quick snack, went on his way with the satchel full of newspapers slung over his shoulder.

Chapter 7

Familiarisation

Jimmy (John from now on) found the paper round fairly undemanding as the area he served was composed largely of rows of Victorian terraced housing, fairly similar to his former home, with the front doors opening directly onto the street. It was only as he reached the outskirts of Elton did he encounter Edwardian villas usually built in blocks of four with neat little front gardens.

Once he had completed his paper round, he quickly doubled back to Martin and Sons, the grocers who Fred had mentioned earlier. On entering the store, John found Amos Martin, the proprietor, deep in conversation with a young girl aged about eleven years. The pair of them were huddled over a huge sack of granulated sugar which was propped up against the shop counter on the serving side. On the counter stood a pair of metal scales with numerous brass weights arranged alongside ranging from one ounce to two pounds. Adjacent to the weights was a huge pile of blue paper bags in varying sizes capable of holding from four ounces to two pounds.

"Now, our Millie, your two brothers have been called up to join the army and you'll have to help me and your mum both in the shop and around the house," said Amos Martin. "Filling these bags isn't hard, you just have to measure correctly and try not to spill any sugar, it's become really precious. There's lots of recipes about now where they're using carrots instead of sugar, believe it or not."

"I don't mind helping at all," replied Millie, "it's boring in the house when you and Mum are in the shop. I can't read all the time; there's not much on the radio for my age and quite a lot of children have been evacuated."

"You're lucky you didn't have to go," answered Amos, "but your dose of measles was so bad that the doctor said you needed to be with your family. Thank goodness you're over it now."

Suddenly, both Amos and Millie realized that they had an audience and halted the conversation to concentrate their attention on the waiting John.

"Now lad, what can we do for you?" questioned Amos.

"My name is John Adams and I'm not here to buy anything at the moment," he replied.

"Well, John, we've nothing to give away," chuckled Amos, followed by Millie's giggles.

"No, I've come about your vacancy for the Saturday job," was John's reply.

"How have you heard about that?" a startled Amos replied. "It's only just something I've been thinking about."

"Fred at the paper shop told me that you probably needed a delivery lad," replied John, "I've just moved into the area and have started marking up and delivering papers for him. I told him that I was also on the lookout for a Saturday job so that's why I'm here."

"Can you ride a bike?" asked Amos, "that's essential for the job that's going."

John swallowed hard and told a double lie, "Yes, course I can. I learned when I lived on a military base with Mum and Dad." This also told Amos that John's dad wasn't around!

"I want you to make up customer's orders and deliver them on the shop bike," continued Amos. "There's no other grocers shop left standing for some distance so it gets really busy and me, the missus, and Millie here will be needed to weigh up and serve. You'd be surprised how busy this little place gets."

"That's not a bike in the back yard, it's a wild animal," interrupted Millie, "I've tried to ride it; the chain tries to bite your ankles, the handlebars do their best to twist out of your hands, and the saddle pinches your bum."

"Shut up, Millie," growled Amos, at his daughter's outburst, "you'll put him off the job."

"No way!" exclaimed John, "I've read all about rodeo riders and bucking broncos so I'm willing to risk it. Anyway, me mum needs the money."

Inside he was virtually quaking as his only cycling experiences had centred on an old three-wheeler when he was seven years old. The thought of having to ride this contrary steed piled high, front and rear, with heavy boxes of groceries was bringing him out in a cold sweat.

John quickly calmed his nerves and continued, "I'm game for anything; can I start this Saturday?"

"Yes, definitely, you're on the team," replied Amos, "you seem keen enough and if Fred's taken you on you must be honest and trustworthy. I'll give you a bob a day to start with and a bit extra on your groceries if you and your mum register your ration books with me." He rubbed his hands together as though they were cold at the thought of gaining another two regular customers.

"Smashing! Thank you very much for the chance," enthused John. "I'll tell you what; if I can borrow the order bike to get used to it I can go home and bring our ration books back here."

"All right," replied Amos, "off you go through the back store room; Millie will come with you and lock the back gate after you've gone."

This last statement disappointed John, for he was hoping his non-existent cycling ability wouldn't be disclosed and that he would have ample practice time in secret. That's what you get for telling lies, he thought, his gran's sayings coming to the fore again. "Give me a thief any time, I can sort them out, but liars I can't figure. Just remember the more porky pies a liar tells, the more chance he has of getting a story wrong and being found out!"

"Come on, dreamboat! I haven't got all day you know." Millie's sharp comment quickly brought John back to reality.

She led him out of the store into the backyard and pointed out the monster. There, standing upright on a telescopic stand was an ancient black bicycle that evidently had seen better days or even years! The vehicle had been adapted to deliver grocery orders. The front wheel was very small to accommodate a metal frame welded to the top of the front fork below the handlebars. This structure allowed cardboard boxes of grocery orders to be stacked inside and roped together to prevent them from toppling sideways. No way could anyone look straight ahead and steer without reducing the pile he was expected to carry. A similar metal frame was welded to the rear forks and sat atop the full-sized wheel. John noticed, with some appre-hension, that there was no chain guard to prevent socks or lower leg parts getting enmeshed if he wasn't particularly careful.

"I thought air raids were bad!" he muttered under his breath, "but at least you could usually hide away fairly safely from them!" There was nowhere to hide, though, from his present predicament.

Millie quickly unlocked the huge padlock, slid back the retaining bars on the gate, and pushed open the creaking door.

"Come on," she said sharply, "get the 'monster' off its stand and away with you. I've got my sugar order to finish off before I start on the butter; it's going to be a long day for me."

John pushed the delivery bicycle off its stand, and, as its weight came as a great surprise, had some difficulty in preventing it from toppling over. He quickly regained his composure and managed to push the bicycle through the open gate and into the back alley.

"I'll just check it over before I ride it!" exclaimed John, sincerely hoping that Millie's other pressing duties would cause her to quickly shut the gate. There was no such luck, though, for John's earlier comments about rodeo riders and bucking broncos had led her to expect a master class in the art of cycling from a fearless exponent!

"Well, get on with it," tutted an expectant Millie, "I'm waiting. You're scared of it, aren't you?" was her scornful comment.

"It certainly needs careful handling," an apprehensive John replied, "and it's a while since I last rode a two-wheeler. Well, here goes." Trusting to luck, he pointed the unwieldy machine down the slight slope, pushed hard, and attempted to lift his right leg over the crossbar. Unfortunately he had misjudged the height of the saddle and caught his ankle a nasty blow on the offending object. Gravity did the rest and he quickly found himself upended on a pile of earth with the bicycle on top of him.

Peals of laughter greeted his efforts as Millie rushed forward to help him. "That was better than the last Laurel and Hardy film I saw at the local cinema," she giggled.

Together they hauled the bicycle back onto its stand and John quickly brushed the soil from his clothing. Apart from an aching ankle and a bruised ego, he was relatively unhurt.

"Wait a minute," ordered Millie, "I'll go and get the bike spanners so you can lower the saddle."

She quickly returned with the spanners and the seat was lowered to the point where John could sit on the saddle and touch the ground with his toes.

"Now off you go," chuckled Millie, "and remember that those cowboys actually got on their horses before they were bucked off!"

John simply grunted in reply, pushed the bicycle down the slope, and successfully mounted. Fortunately the bicycle had recently been fitted with a three-speed gear system operated by a trigger mechanism on the handlebars adjacent to one of the brake handles. This upgrading to the pedalling system was a great aid and he quickly found the lowest gear. This action enabled the pedals to move around furiously with the minimum of effort whilst the bicycle moved at a sedate speed, enabling him to concentrate on the steering.

As it was still fairly early and there was no fixed time limit to return to the grocery store, John spent the rest of the morning taming the beast. Eventually, much later in the day, a triumphant but exhausted John returned the bicycle to the premises along with the two Adams ration books!

Chapter 8

An Educational Shock!

The following morning, John delivered his newspapers and returned to his hideaway. Now was the time to realize all his assets and he started by carefully adjusting the curtains to allow rays of light to penetrate the room thus saving him the cost of an electric light! He started with the wardrobe, which contained several items of ladies clothing and shoes that John Adams's mum had been unable to pack into the one small suitcase allowed for each person boarding the ship. He pushed the ladies apparel to one end of the wardrobe and continued with his search. The remainder of the wardrobe revealed a veritable treasure trove of shirts and trousers. The shelves contained underwear, handkerchiefs, socks, and shoes—all suitable for his size.

John considered that he had been very lucky with his search so far, but was quickly brought back down-to-earth when he opened the top drawer of the dressing table. The drawer contained a letter addressed to Mr. and Mrs. Adams concerning their son John's entrance on a free scholarship to Acres Hill Grammar School in mid-September, now less than two weeks away. There had been no eleven-plus examinations at Jimmy Atkins School that year, for the bombing raids had totally disrupted educational procedures in the Milton area of Shrimport. In fact, his school had secondary provision up to the age of fourteen years (the normal school leaving age) and plans were already being drawn up to transfer the more educationally gifted into the town's grammar and junior technical/commercial schools at the first opportunity.

John now contemplated the fact that he had gained entry to a high-flying educational institution without knowing if he was capable of achieving the rigorous standards demanded. Whilst the thoughts of much study and regular homework were a worry in themselves, the sheet accompanying the letter caused him to gasp in horror for it read as follows:

Each student is required to attend Acres Hill Grammar School regularly and punctually on school days. Furthermore, students should be clean and smart of person and always be attired in the school uniform. They should also be polite and respectful to all adults encountered on the way to school and also on leaving it at the end of normal classroom hours.

In the case of boys, each family should purchase the following from Whittle's Emporium, High Street, Shrimport, who is the only stockist of the school uniform and associated equipment:

- 1 school cap
- 3 pairs of short grey trousers
- 1 school blazer
- 3 long sleeved white shirts
- 1 school tie
- 2 pairs of white gym shorts
- 3 pairs of long grey socks
- 1 pair of black plimsolls
- 1 school soccer shirt
- 1 school satchel
- 1 pair of school soccer stockings
- 1 pair of black shoes
- 1 pair of soccer boots
- The school will supply the requisite text and exercise books, but each student should be equipped with the following:
- 1 12-inch ruler and protractor set
- 1 fountain pen and ink
- Various coloured pencils

All pupils are required to have lunch at school and are requested to bring with them on each Monday morning the sum of one shilling and eight pence (1/8d) to cover the cost of a week's meals.

John was now faced with a major dilemma; he would need at least ten pounds to buy all the necessary items along with the further complication of purchasing them without a parent or guardian being present!

A much-deflated John continued his search, refusing to be cheered by the stock of boy's clothing he had uncovered. The kitchen shelves revealed a selection of pots, pans, crockery, and cutlery, plus two tins of beans and one of soup.

John sat on one of the dining chairs with his head in his hands. He felt very low; was this the end of his bid to stay out of the orphanage after all his endeavours? Would he have to march into Shrimport Town Hall and declare that Jimmy Atkins had returned from the dead?

Desperate times meant desperate measures and, after wiping away the odd tear, John concentrated on his predicament and, some time later, he had made a note of three possible solutions to his financial shortcomings, two of which were fraught with danger!

The first and easiest, which presented little trouble, just nerve, he carried out almost immediately. Quickly bundling together most of the items of female clothing and footwear, he hurried off to find a special shop. The premises he headed for had an unusual sign outside, namely three brass balls. It was known as the pawnbroker. The proprietor would purchase any item you wished to sell and issue you with a special ticket enabling you to buy back your items at a slightly higher price within a certain time limit. The items you sold (or pawned) were said to be in hock!

John had seen a pawnbroker's shop strategically situated close to the town docks where visiting ship's crews could quickly raise extra funds by selling exotic items bought cheaply abroad. He quickly traversed a route to his destination that carefully avoided his old haunts of Milton and entered the shop.

The proprietor was well-used to dealing with children as some of the adjoining streets contained families not averse to pawning items on Monday after a weekend's merry making had used up all their funds. They usually bought the items back on Friday evening after the weekly wage had been tipped up.

John's items of clothing and footwear were clean, fashionable, and of particular interest to the pawnbroker. After some protracted haggling, he left the shop over one pound richer.

The next business would take place after dark so he returned home for some tea.

Chapter 9

A Harrowing Encounter

As John ate his beans on toast, followed by an apple, he thumbed through the two ration books he had placed on the dining table. The books belonged to Jimmy Atkins and his grandma, now both classed as being dead! He realised that there was no way he could use them any more as it would simply heighten the chance of being discovered. He had a good idea who could! Up until now, John had only told lies and sold off clothes and footwear that were surplus to requirements. The next step he was contemplating would make him a criminal, an act which made the normally honest and forthright boy feel very uncomfortable.

The reason he was waiting for darkness was that he was going to return to a particular part of the dockside area where various shady characters operated! They were known locally as spivs, or more commonly, black marketeers. The spivs obtained, by fair means or foul, all manner of goods that were rationed or in short supply and would sell them at inflated prices to all comers. The police did not look too kindly on these nefarious activities, but the under-strength force already had far too much to contend with to stamp out the practices.

For their part, the spivs had lookouts placed at strategic positions who could quickly signal the approach of any lawman, at which point the lawbreakers would quickly disappear.

Dusk arrived and John plucked up his courage and went to deal with these shady characters. At this point he felt really lonely and scared, for although he had never dealt with these lawbreakers before, he had heard enough stories about them in the school playground to know how unscrupulous they could be. He decided to take as little chances as possible, so after putting one ration book in his trouser pocket, he carefully secreted the other one under his shirt.

John made his way to the dockside and the fitful moon-light showed him one of the spivs lounging against the dock gates.

"Hello, sonny," grunted the spiv, "what brings the likes of you down here at this time o'night? Is the pawn shop shut?"

"Wh-What I-I've got for you isn't for the pawn shop," stammered John, trying desperately to overcome his nervousness. He was uncomfortably aware that a lookout wasn't too far away.

"Come on lad, what've you got to sell me? Quick now, time's money you know," rasped the spiv, keeping one furtive eye on John and the other for any signal from his lookout that meant the approach of any policeman.

"It's a full ration book belonging to someone who sailed to Canada the other day," the lie tumbling from John's lips.

"Blimey," chortled the spiv, moving eagerly towards John, "come on then, lad, let's see the colour of it?"

"Wh-What will you give me for it?" stuttered a still nervous John.

"How about thirty-bob?" chirped the spiv.

"I-I think it's worth a lot more than that," carried on John, a note of desperation beginning to creep into his voice as he sensed some movement nearby and was sure someone was sneaking up on him.

"Grab him, Nobby, he's on his own!" shouted the spiv.

"Got him," grunted the spiv's accomplice as he grabbed John by the arm and made to search him with the other hand.

"No you haven't!" squawked John as he quickly back-heeled the accomplice in the shins and wriggled out of the howling Nobby's grasp. He quickly sprinted away from the danger area. As he did so, he heard Nobby's voice full of rage.

"I'll get you for that, you little perisher," shrieked Nobby as he hobbled away.

There was little chase, as it could possibly alert the law, so he was soon able to slow down and take a breather. Although he was badly shaken by events, he felt gratified that he hadn't broken the law and no longer felt a criminal. It was a relieved John who reached the safety of his apartment and settled down for the night, even though he hadn't made a successful sale.

Chapter 10

Buried Treasure!

Saturday dawned bright and clear and John was both pleased and relieved to get back to his newspaper marking up and delivery. He then made his way to the grocery store to start his second job.

After being introduced to Mrs. Martin, a practical, no-nonsense lady, who quickly disappeared to the upstairs accommodation, John loaded up his bicycle and began his muscle-aching delivery round.

As he pedalled along, his mind was dwelling on his cash problem and the final solution to alleviate it. His plan was to return to the ruin of his former home for there was buried treasure there!

Because of his other pressing problems he'd faced, he had initially forgotten about his grandma's savings. She had always maintained that the safest place to retire to in the event of an air raid was in the cubbyhole under the stairs. On more than one occasion John had shared this cramped accommodation with his grandma whilst the bombs had rained down on Shrimport. The terraced houses were very old and the builder had covered the kitchen area and cubbyhole with stone flagstones rather than wooden boards.

Thomas Atkins, before he left for France, had, at grandma's insistence, carefully chiselled the mortar from the perimeter of one of the flagstones in the cubbyhole. He had then scooped out the soil and rubble from the centre of the filling to leave a crater wide and deep enough for an old biscuit tin to be inserted. In the receptacle went the family's insurance policies, some pieces of jewellery, and a bag of mixed notes and coins; all grandma's savings for a rainy day.

John was certain that the secure location of this buried treasure could survive anything but a direct hit from a bomb. Also, anyone searching the rubble of the ruined house would have no idea what was buried there. What complicated matters somewhat was that, as often as possible, regular patrols of the home guard or special constables kept watch on newly bombed-out houses to prevent any looters from taking anything of value remaining amongst the wreckage. Most of the volunteer soldiers of the home guard were retired veterans from the Boer and First World Wars, and whose reflexes were far from sharp. The platoon was boosted by a number of teenagers eagerly awaiting their call-up to the armed forces. No way could John hope to outrun these fit young lads if he was spotted.

The special constables (who supplemented the police force) largely consisted of men between twenty-one and fifty years old who were in reserved occupations, that is their skills were vital to the war effort. This group spent long hours in the factories producing munitions to replace those lost at Dunkirk.

All of these two groups took their security work very seriously and woe betide any looters who fell into their hands. 'He fell over, banged his head, and injured his ribs!' were written comments against many names in the arrests book.

Luckily for John, he had made a discovery on one of the shelves under the sink. He had been attempting to push the smaller pans further on their shelf when he had noticed a long, thin wooden box positioned behind the utensils. The box was actually preventing the saucepans from sitting more comfortably on the shelf. It contained several candles, a box of safety matches, and, most important of all with regards to his quest, a small torch with two spare batteries. These items were a necessity in every household as air raids could easily knock out gas and electricity supplies for days at a time; therefore, any source of alternative lighting was carefully hoarded.

The timing of his visit to his former home had to be just right to lessen his chances of being caught. What he desperately needed was another night air raid. Most security patrols would stay in the air raid shelters until the all-clear was sounded. This meant that John, to achieve his objective, would have to brave an air raid out in the open, a terrifying and unnerving task for any adult, never mind an eleven year old, however feisty.

John hadn't long to wait, for at dusk on the moonless Saturday evening the air raid sirens sounded and he quickly slipped out into the darkness, taking with him the precious torch and his canvas shopping bag to hold, hopefully, the prized biscuit tin.

As an added precaution, John had rescued an old brown envelope from the newsagent's wastepaper bin. He had carefully stuck pieces of the gummed portion around the perimeter of the torch's prism. Only a very narrow beam of light could then penetrate the darkness. He had copied this action from seeing cars being driven in the dark with most of their headlights being obscured by brown paper being glued across them and a small hole cut in the centre.

On any other blackout evening John could have picked his way through the town by walking on the pavement, being careful to avoid the gutted gas lamp standards and extinguished electricity poles, but this occasion was very different. John wished to attract as little attention as possible, so he continually dodged from one extra darkened spot to another.

By the time he had reached his bomb-blasted street, the air raid had started and bombs were falling on the dockside and nearby factories. Shrapnel from the anti-aircraft batteries positioned around the town was pattering down like grotesque hailstones all around him. The shrapnel caused John some concern, for the hot, twisted lumps of metal could cause serious injuries, especially if they were to hit his unprotected head.

The fact that only three houses on each side of the street had been destroyed made it slightly easier for John to identify his former home, and he was thankful that the larger pieces of rubble had been piled to one side in the hunt for any possible survivors. His grandma had been proved right, for the only portion of the house left standing was the lower part of the staircase which covered a small area of the cubbyhole. Unfortunately, for once, she had been unable to reach this comparatively safe spot and had died as a result.

John slowly and warily approached his goal, the narrow beam of light from his torch guiding him through the smaller debris. He felt his excitement rise. Just as everything seemed to be going right, it happened!! A stray bomb plunged into the deserted street and exploded with a tremendous roar. The blast flung John under the gutted remains of the staircase, which protected him from the flying rubble but knocked him cold for some minutes.

"Somebody up there or somewhere else doesn't seem to like me," he muttered to himself as slowly but surely his senses returned.

Scrabbling around, he followed the narrow beam of light and located his torch. He positioned the light so that it shone on the loose flagstone atop the treasure, placed his fingers either side and tried to lift it, but, to his consternation, it refused to budge. After several fruitless attempts to lift the flagstone, he realized that he did not have the necessary strength and sat back in dismay. To make matters even worse, the all clear siren began to wail and John realised the security patrols would soon start again. Bombs had fallen in the vicinity and they would be making a beeline for the street along with the fire and rescue services.

"Got it," he whispered to himself, "if I slip a crowbar under the edge of the flagstone I can lever it up and swing it to one side; but what can I use to help me?" He began scrabbling amidst the debris to see if he could find the right tool for the job and, at this point, his luck turned for the better.

The kitchen sink had been supported by a cast iron frame and sticking out of a pile of rubble was one of its metal legs. John slowly pulled the leg from the debris, trying to minimise the noise and avoiding a landslide of displaced brickwork and plaster. He quickly placed the sharp end of the leg under the edge of the loosened flagstone and leaned hard on the other end of his lever. Very slowly and reluctantly, the edge of the flagstone began to rise. Not daring to let go of his crowbar John used his foot to push some small pieces of house brick under the raised edge. He then loosened his grip on the lever and allowed the flagstone to settle on his quickly-fashioned wedge. After pausing for breath and gathering several larger pieces of masonry to act as additional wedges, he raised the flagstone higher and built brick supporting columns under its edge and side. He was now able to re-position the lever and, with much effort and grunting, he began to push the heavy flagstone sideways, completely out of its old alignment. Eventually it toppled down with a crash that seemed, to the sweating and exhausted boy, to echo for miles around in the now much-quieter night!

John now heard voices in the distance and realized that his noisy activity had attracted attention. He re-positioned his torch and shone it into the hole and a jubilant John was now able to see the biscuit tin thinly outlined against a screen of dust.

Grabbing the treasure trove he stuffed it into his canvas bag and made to move out of the derelict ruin.

By now there was definite movement in the street and rescue teams began the unenviable task of trying to locate any survivors from the newly demolished houses. John's excitement at recovering the biscuit tin was now tempered by the fact that he still wasn't safe from discovery and he resisted the temptation to make a run for it. Instead he moved slowly and carefully trying desperately to avoid the shards of glass, of which the crunching underfoot would certainly attract attention.

Again luck was with him as he heard the leader of the rescue team address his crew as follows: "There's nothing to look for in the middle of the street. Those houses were hit in the last big raid. Concentrate your efforts on the fresh lot of wreckage at the top end."

Because of his slow and careful progress, it was some time before the dark shapes of the trees in the park became visible. John now blessed his good fortune again, for he was able to mingle with people as they emerged from the air raid shelter that had been his former saviour. It was then just a matter of being cautious and watching out for any likely trouble as he made his triumphant way back to his then-home.

Chapter 11

A Good Deed and a Chink in His Armour

The following morning, John made his way to the newsagent's, happy in the knowledge that his major financial difficulties were behind him for some time. He had carefully prised back the bath panel and secreted the biscuit tin there hoping that it was now in a new and equally secure hiding place.

He had also taken the precaution of totally surveying the whole of the desolate area around the former car showroom and was satisfied that he was the only occupant for several blocks. This did not stop him opening the door extremely carefully and examining the area before leaving. Most of the time the only onlookers were seagulls or the odd stray dog or cat. Another precaution he had taken was to vary his route to and from home to avoid possible detection.

Fred, the newsagent, was in a particularly grumpy mood when John arrived for his morning's work.

"That storeroom's a right mess," moaned Fred, "should have sorted it out ages ago but kept putting it off."

"Can I help you after I've finished my paper round?" asked John, "I've only got to go to Whittle's Emporium for my grammar school uniform and stuff and I can easily do that this afternoon."

"Good lad!" exclaimed Fred, visibly cheered up by this offer of help, "after we've finished you can have your lunch with me and there'll be extra in your pay packet come the end of the week."

With the prospect of more income from the additional effort, John set to his marking up with a will and delivered his newspapers with an extra spring in his step.

Later that morning, Fred and John set to work on the storeroom. With two pairs of hands, the task seemed less onerous. Rubbish was swiftly identified and removed, and before long order began to emerge from the chaos. Eventually all that was left to be investigated was a large tin trunk. Fred opened the creaking lid and exclaimed, "Just look at this lot?" John gasped in amazement for the trunk contained a multi-coloured assortment of fireworks. There were rockets, roman candles, jumping jacks, catherine wheels, and a wide selection of bangers. "I'm saving these for when there's something good to celebrate," said Fred, "goodness knows how long that will be with this dratted war dragging on. Tell you what, you take a selection then you can celebrate as well. I might not make it."

"Ooh, thanks," gasped John, whose last experience of fireworks had been November 5, 1938, Guy Fawkes Night. He had been compelled to watch adults lighting a small number of cheap and irregularly performing pyrotechnics whilst he and the other children waved sparklers around. He had certainly enjoyed his grandma's home-made treacle toffee, but had never been particularly fond of the older boys' contribution to the evening. These children insisted on roasting poorly washed potatoes in the glowing embers of the bonfire, which were then passed around the youngsters. These treats were totally charred and blackened on the outside whilst being almost raw in the middle.

Fred passed a large, strong, brown paper carrier bag to John, who carefully selected a range of fireworks from the ample supply in the trunk. He was also instructed to include some of the slow-burning strings used to light the blue touch papers.

After lunch with Fred, John retuned home with his precious cargo. Once he had safely deposited his parcel, he left to buy his school uniform.

Whittle's Emporium was the grandest shop in the high street and the only department store in the town that was still operating. Mr. George, the grandson of the founder, was a large imposing figure and one of the town's senior councillors; he was also a governor of Acres Hill Grammar School. He had continued to expand the family business and purchased substantial premises either side of the original store. There were now three separate departments for men, women, and children as well as a general section.

John could hardly suppress a grin as he approached the portly store owner who was patrolling the pavement outside the store's main lobby. Mr. George was dressed in a pin stripe suit and a bowler hat, carrying a large, rolled-up umbrella which he brandished like a sword, with the obligatory gas mask swinging at his hip. It was as though he was daring Hitler himself to threaten his business!

Seeing John's hesitation, for he had never entered the store before, Mr. George strode towards him.

"Now young man," he boomed, "what can Whittle's Emporium do for you?"

John quickly produced the letter from Acres Hill Grammar School and handed it to Mr. George.

"Ah, another of the future's captains of industry and commerce come to dress the Whittle way," roared Mr. George, "come with me lad, I'll personally escort you to the right department."

An embarrassed John was quickly marched into the store and eventually deposited in front of a severe, elderly sales lady who gazed at him over horn-rimmed glasses.

"Miss Agnes, I leave this precious cargo in your more than capable hands," purred Mr. George, and he went on his way.

For her part, Miss Agnes' eyes misted over as she regarded the retreating figure of Mr. George.

"What a man!" she sighed, and then, on realising that a boy was staring at her wide-eyed, quickly became her professional self.

"Now then, young man, I see you've got your grammar school letter with you; is there anything on the list you have already?"

"Yes," answered John, "I've got some black shoes but that's all."

"Come on then, John," said Miss Agnes, reading his name on the letter, "just follow me round and we'll pick up the necessary items."

They moved quickly around the various counters, picking up the items on the list as they went. Eventually they paused in front of the changing cubicles.

"Just pop in here and make sure that everything is all right," chirped Miss Agnes.

John had hardly swished the curtains closed when Millie Martin and her mother appeared in the room with handfuls of female apparel in Acres Hill Grammar School colours.

"I've just got to pick up my parcel from the ladies department," Mrs. Martin addressed Millie, "by the time you have tried on all your clothes I'll be back."

Millie dutifully entered a changing cubicle.

A short time passed and John emerged from his cubicle to the waiting Miss Agnes.

"Did I choose correctly, John Adams?" questioned Miss Agnes, a matter of personal pride to the long-time store assistant!

"Yes, everything is fine," gulped John, who was wishing himself a thousand miles from his present predicament.

Millie, in her changing cubicle, pricked up her ears at the mention of the name and, in particular, the answer given.

"Well it's not every day an eleven-year-old boy comes in here unaccompanied and needs to be fitted out. I assume Dad's away and Mum's on shift work at one of the factories," queried Miss Agnes.

"That's right," answered John, "Mum's far too busy at work and she knew that I would be well looked after at Whittles."

"Come on then, John, let's go to the pay desk and get this lot wrapped up, clothing coupons torn out, and paid for," answered a beaming Miss Agnes at the compliment that had come her way.

They left the department and moved to the central foyer.

A short time after they had left, Millie emerged from her changing cubicle with a puzzled look on her face.

"It's very odd," she muttered to herself, "John told my dad that his mum was too poorly to work much and yet he has just told a saleslady that she was too busy working to come to the store with him. I'm going to keep an eye on him!"

Just then, Mrs. Martin appeared carrying her parcel and Millie pushed her thoughts to the back of her mind for the moment as she concentrated on equipping herself for the grammar school.

Chapter 12

An Unwelcome Lodger

It was Saturday evening and John had successfully completed his grocery and paper rounds. He carried home his tea; a cheap and nourishing meal of fish, chips, and peas wrapped up in a newspaper. He treated himself to this ration-free delicacy twice per week, thankful that it reduced his home cooking which, although previously encouraged by his grandma, tended to be of the all-in-one pot variety!

Once his meal was completed, he considered his next task, that of washing his clothes. This consisted of dropping all the grubby items into his bath water along with some washing powder and letting the items steep overnight. There was no iron available in the rooms and John's answer to this problem had been to let the washing dry by hanging out the wrung-out clothes on a line over the bath. He then put the most badly creased items under the mattress on the bed and slept on them! So far this method had worked reasonably well but how to appear clean, tidy, and fully presentable when he attended Acres Hill Grammar School was causing him some concern.

His domestic chores completed for the evening, John tumbled into bed hoping for a good night's rest before his Sunday morning newspaper duties. Hardly an hour had passed before the air raid siren sounded and the boom of the anti-aircraft guns reverberated around the room. John was too tired to move, however, and was pleasantly surprised to hear the all clear sound shortly afterwards without the noise of any bombs exploding.

John woke with a start; it wasn't yet dawn, but he had had been disturbed by a ripping, creaking noise that appeared to be coming from the downstairs showroom.

"Oh no," he muttered, "that noise probably means I've got company below. I bet some old tramp's spied out this place and is settling in for the winter. There's no way I can let him do that, for he'll soon realize that somebody is living upstairs. How long after that before my secret's out? Never mind now. There's nothing I can do about it until later tomorrow."

He still managed to turn over and go to sleep, but not before he had put the alarm clock under his pillow to reduce the sound of its early morning clarion call!

The following morning John crept around the room as quietly as possible, not even daring to flush the lavatory or turn on the taps. A lick and a spit with the wet flannel was all his hands and face got before he left for the newsagent's. On arriving there, he was greeted by an exultant Fred.

"Guess what?" he cried, fairly hopping up and down in his enthusiasm, "only one plane came over to bomb Shrimport last night and our gallant gunners did for him. The aircraft went down in flames over the sea just after the crew bailed out. The home guard quickly nailed most of 'em, although they reckon the pilot is still unaccounted for. Apparently he was the last to leave the plane and some people reckon they saw what looked like a parachute dropping down. They reckoned it could have landed near here, in the bombed-out part of Elton, but you know how rumours spread. For all we are aware, he went down with his plane."

John paled at the last disclosure, realizing the true implication of what had woken him in the night. *Oh no, he didn't drown in the sea*, he thought, *he did land in Elton and he's now my near neighbour*!

Once again he was faced with a serious quandary. If he reported the matter to the security services, they would be bound to ask awkward questions about his family circumstances. Also, horror of horrors, the press would want to interview the young hero and possibly print his story, and photograph, in the local newspaper. In that case, he was bound to be recognised and the game would be up.

All these thoughts were going through his head as he made his paper round and still occupied his mind as the day wore on.

It was only after he had finished a cold evening meal, constructed as quietly as possible, that a plan began to form. Once again he had to wait until the onset of darkness before he began to take the necessary action to oust his very unwelcome neighbour.

John carefully crept downstairs in the deepening gloom, carrying with him the weirdest collection of objects. Carefully stuffed in his pockets were two penny banger fireworks and a skyrocket. Roped across his shoulders, like an ancient long-bow, was a broom handle. In his hands were an empty milk bottle, a saucepan, and a lighted slow-burning string.

Earlier in the day he had closely reconnoitred the shuttered showroom and made careful note of which of the wooden boards had been forced for the airman to gain entry. He made his way to the spot and began to put his plan into action. Finding some level ground, he deposited the milk bottle and placed the skyrocket inside. Next, he lit one of the penny bangers and put it as near to the forced shutter as possible.

Bang! The noise seemed tremendous to John, and he could only imagine the consternation it must have caused to the airman in the showroom.

"Hands hoch," boomed John into the depths of the sauce-pan, fervently hoping his voice sounded adult, also that his knowledge of the German language, gleaned from war films at his local cinema would suffice. "Raus, raus, com en ze 'ere!" he shouted. "The next bullet is for you!"

With a screech, the wooden barrier was pushed to one side and a shocked airman stumbled out into the darkness, quickly putting his hands over his head.

John stepped behind the flier and prodded him in the small of his back with the broom handle.

"Quick march," he boomed into the saucepan, before lowering it to the ground and applying the slow match to the touch paper of the rocket. With a *whoosh* the rocket climbed vertically into the sky and exploded with a loud bang.

It seemed an eternity, but was only a short time before a home guard patrol appeared to find a bewildered, but unaccompanied, German airman standing in the open with his hands over his head. John had disappeared into the darkness as soon as he heard the voices of the patrol coming to investigate this strange phenomenon.

"All right, Jerry, consider yourself under arrest and locked up for the duration!" exclaimed the elderly platoon corporal. "I'll be darned how you've come to be here like this, but you're captured now and that's all that counts."

Once the prisoner and patrol had moved off into the darkness, John secured the wooden barrier as best he could before he retreated up the stairs.

Chapter 13

School

It was with a deep feeling of trepidation that John approached the imposing buildings of Acres Hill Grammar School. As the name suggested, the pile stood on what amounted for a hill in the largely flat town of Shrimport.

The school was constructed of grey stone and was two storeys high. At one end was a substantial hall, well capable of holding the five-hundred-plus pupils and staff. There was an imposing stage at one end that could hold a fairly large orchestra or choir. It was also used for plays. A well-stocked library occupied the other end of the building, and sandwiched between were a variety of classrooms, cloakrooms, staff rooms, and specialist laboratories. Connected at the rear of the main building was a covered passageway leading to a recently completed two-storey, woodwork, domestic science block, and a state-of-the-art gymnasium.

The original classrooms dated from the early seventeenth century and the school was proud of its traditions originally in the arts, but increasingly in the sciences as well. It maintained strong links with both Oxford and Cambridge Universities and the staff and governors prided themselves on sending a steady stream of first-rate students to a wide range of higher educational institutions.

The yearly intake to the school was a maximum of ninety-six pupils divided into three classes. The vast majority of the students were fee-paying pupils with approximately ten percent free scholarship admissions. A two-year sixth form was made up of around fifty pupils who were regarded with due awe and respect by the younger members of the school. Twelve each of the senior boys and girls were prefects who linked closely with the teachers to maintain a high level of discipline throughout the school.

In an attempt to encourage teamwork, co-operation and pride in belonging the school was divided into four houses. To reflect the growing influence of science and technology, they were called Stephenson (colour red), Brunel (green), Cavendish (yellow), and Newton (blue), each with a housemaster and a proportion of prefects.

The headmaster, an old Oxfordian, had, very wisely, instigated a procedure that involved the new entrants along with the academic staff and prefects attending the school one day ahead of the rest of the other pupils.

After the initial address to the new entrants, the headmaster introduced the staff, who were mainly middle-aged or past retirement. The latter group had returned to the school as part of the war effort, freeing up younger members of staff to join the armed forces or participate in more secret matters.

The assembly was then divided into quarters, and each group of twelve boys and a similar number of girls was marched off to different classrooms to be introduced to the staff and prefects controlling each of the four houses. John, along with Millie, found himself in Brunel house, ruled over by a science teacher called Mr. Foster. This housemaster prided himself on instilling into his charges all the best virtues that constituted the make-up of an English lady or gentleman.

The housemaster's address to the new entrants was both stirring and sincere as befitted a country attempting to come to terms with the parlous situation it faced. Little was needed to remind the children, who were veterans of many bombing raids and some recently returned from evacuation, that the enemy was only some thirty miles or so from England's south coast. In particular, the youngsters were instructed to study closely the paintings which decorated the school's corridors at specific intervals. The brushwork may have been fairly insignificant but, by and large, most were particularly gruesome depictions from the past three hundred years of British history. Prevalent were the death scenes showing Wolfe at Quebec, Nelson at Trafalgar, and Sir John Moore before Corunna. Equally traumatic was a picture of Captain Oates staggering from a tent into the teeth of an Antarctic blizzard during the ill-fated expedition to the South Pole, entitled *A Very Gallant Gentleman*!

Shortly after the house rules had been explained, a prim, precise lady entered the classroom. After introducing herself as the school secretary, the lady proceeded to read out names and classroom numbers so the three forms could be assembled to meet their tutor and receive text and exercise books. John, Millie, and thirty other pupils found themselves allocated to form 1B whilst others went to 1A or 1C. Their form tutor was a firm, elderly lady called Miss Curry, who seemed to the youngsters to be everyone's grandma. She was also their history teacher, a subject she taught with real passion and feeling.

After introducing herself to the class, she despatched John and another boy to bring in crates of milk for the morning break. Straws were carefully doled out to drink the milk from the bottles and the students were asked to bring to school a glass or beaker as milk receptacles, thus saving the use of straws!

After drinking the milk, the students were allowed a fifteen-minute break and filed quietly out into the playground areas, separate for boys and girls. John found himself alone, for all the other boys seemed to be from private preparatory schools scattered around Shrimport. Their parents had been paying school fees since the children were five years old and had grown up together. The fee-payers seemed to have congregated into groups according to their prep schools.

Suddenly, John's attention was drawn to a commotion in the furthest corner of the playground where a group of five boys surrounded a small youngster who seemed to be cowering by the wall. The group, all from 1B, led by a tubby florid-faced boy called Donald Cowper, were taunting the boy, pushing him, and calling him names.

John, who abhorred bullying, moved towards the group to see if he could help. Suddenly, the small boy who had seemed to be crouching down with his face turned towards the wall, turned on his attackers and lashed out. To John's surprise he realized that he was looking at a Chinese youngster, the first he had seen in Shrimport. Adult Chinese were common in the seaport with cargo ships coming from all over the world, but not children.

The small boy's quick movement caught the taunting group by surprise and his fist connected with Cowper's nose. With a howl of anguish, the bully fell backwards as blood spilled onto his pristine white shirt.

"Bash him, Don," yelled one of the gang as the group grabbed the young boy's arms and legs. "Sort him out good and proper! You can't let scholarship kids get away with that," shrieked another.

Things were looking really ominous for the young Chinese when John spoke up.

"Let him go or you'll have to deal with me as well," he roared, "we scholarship kids stick together too, you know."

The young bullies paused in their endeavours, which allowed the tormented boy to wriggle free of his captors and swiftly move to John's side.

"Keep out of this if you know what's good for you," growled Cowper, through the folds of his blood-soaked handkerchief.

"Why should I?" grated John, his blood well and truly up; for though he was never one to start a fight, he'd certainly taken part in his share in the past six years. "I see you're not so keen on scrapping now there's two of us."

The outcome of the confrontation was not to be resolved, for at this point, one of the Cowper gang suddenly yelled out, "Prefect coming! Scatter!"

Within seconds, the gang had disappeared from the scene, endeavouring to lose themselves amongst the other groups in the playground. "We'll get both of you for this," was Cowper's final remark as he made off.

"Any trouble here?" queried a quizzical prefect, wondering where the crowd had gone.

"None at all," a cheery John replied, "we were just getting to know one another."

The prefect continued on his patrol and the Chinese boy turned to John. "Thank you very much for helping me," he said, "it could have got very bad for you too I'm sure," the grateful youngster added. "It was very brave of you to stand up to them like that."

"You didn't do too badly yourself," chuckled John, "that right hook you threw was worthy of a heavyweight champion; are you all right now?"

"I'm fine; by the way my name's Freddie Wong, what's yours?"

"John Adams. Pleased to meet you," our hero replied as the two of them shook hands.

"My mum and dad run the Chinese laundry in Elton," Freddie went on, "they've been in England since I was about three, so I speak Cantonese, Mandarin, and English."

"Blimey!" exclaimed John in an awed voice, "I'm in the same class as a genius!"

"Oh no!" exclaimed Freddie, "my best subject is mathematics and my parent's had me coached in that subject since I was seven."

John swallowed hard at this statement, realizing that academic life might be even tougher than he had imagined. *Still*, he thought, *I can only do my best.* Then he visibly brightened as he realised that here was another opportunity that would remove some of his worries.

"Does your laundry take very small orders?" he enquired.

"We take anything and everything that can be washed and ironed," was the reply.

"That's great!" a relieved John answered. "My mum has great difficulty ironing and I'd like to see my shirts looking as good as yours."

"I can certainly see your problem," replied Freddie, wincing as he noticed the creases in John's shirt. "I'm sure that they'll give you a special price for proving to be such a good friend."

Just then the bell sounded for the end of break and the pair moved back to their classroom, chattering away as though they had known each other for years.

Eventually lunchtime arrived and it was a relieved John who sat down to a hot, palatable meal which was satisfying, even if it wasn't up to his grandma's standards. Most certainly it saved him the job of preparing a hot meal for most of the week. The rest of the school day seemed to pass in a blur and it was an exultant youngster who tumbled into bed that evening. He had survived his first day in the new environment and was keenly looking forward to seeing how he would cope as he balanced his demanding schedule of schoolwork, homework, and his two part-time jobs.

Chapter 14

A Dirty Trick

Thanks to the previous day's initiation at school, with all pupils present, it was not so traumatic. There were still some new major rules to be observed; for instance, the kitchens and dining area in their separate wooden building could only cope with a maximum of three hundred staff and pupils at any one time, so sittings were staggered. The girls were allowed thirty minutes on first sitting with the boys following on. The remaining break time was spent outdoors in good weather, and in designated classrooms in inclement conditions.

At the head of each lunch table were at least two sixth-formers who had a mixture of students from each of the lower five years under their control. It was in the dining room that an aspect of fagging took place. The new boys allocated to each table had to carry large trays of plates from the serving area to their respective tables and present the food to their colleagues.

Fortunately, John and Freddie had been allocated to the same table and quickly made themselves known to the older boys. Freddie was subject to some good-natured ribbing about chopsticks but the senior boys ensured that no bullying took place.

It was a largely uneventful meal until the fags were despatched to bring back the puddings. Freddie, concentrating on holding steady a tray filled with pudding dishes of jam roly-poly and custard, failed to notice an obstacle in his path. Donald Cowper, sitting at a table with one of his cronies adjacent to the serving hatch, had already delivered his dishes and, ensuring that he was unobserved, craftily pushed his empty tray into the path of the unsuspecting Freddie. With his view of the floor blocked by the tray he was carrying, he placed one of his feet on the slippery object and crashed down. Pandemonium broke loose as several boys were spattered with roly-poly and custard. It was some time before teachers and prefects restored order.

A crestfallen Freddie was escorted to the first aid room to be checked over whilst sympathetic dinner ladies quickly mopped up the mess and sponged down any affected clothing. Luckily, there was enough spare food to ensure the spoiled puddings were replaced.

John made note of the satisfied grin on Cowper's face and realized that the fracas was no accident. *Freddie and I have made real enemies of the Cowper gang*, he thought, *we'll have to be on our guard against them in future.*

Freddie had not sustained any serious injuries following his fall and was able to join John and Millie as they entered class that afternoon.

"What does that fat boy keep smirking at you for and giving those other lads the thumbs-up sign?" enquired a bemused Millie.

"They've already picked on Freddie in the playground and then, today, caused him to trip up while he was carrying a tray of puddings," replied John.

"I've already heard them sneering about the school's standards being let down by raggedy scholarship kids. I'm sure they were pointing at you, John," Millie went on.

John's face crimsoned in embarrassment as Millie looked pointedly at his creased shirt. "Me mum has difficulty ironing," he explained, "she does the best she can in her condition. Anyway, Wong's Laundry will be taking over that duty shortly."

Freddie, overhearing this last remark, nodded his approval.

"It's a pity she can't work much," carried on Millie relentlessly, determined to see if John confirmed her suspicions.

"Yes, it's a long story," sighed John, as though reluctant to go into more detail.

Just then the teacher entered the classroom and spared John further explanation.

Millie, for her part, sat down frowning deeply, now doubly determined to get to the bottom of this mystery.

By the end of the afternoon school, the students had been given their first homework assignments and went on their way. For his part, John made a beeline for the substantial branch of the town's library service that was situated in Elton. The subject matter was not too taxing at this stage and John quickly finished his tasks. As he was putting his completed work in his satchel, he thought of a plan to save him time and effort and, most importantly, money. "I'll come here from school every day," he muttered to himself, "I can do my homework and go straight to the newsagent's to do my evening round. Fred will let me keep some old clothes there to change into so I can protect my school uniform. After my paper round I can go home for tea and it means I don't have to use either gas or electricity till late on."

School swiftly developed into a routine and John, Freddie, and Millie—the only scholarship children in Form 1B— quickly became firm friends. Both the other two soon joined John on his afternoon visits to the branch library. Although John enjoyed their company, he was becoming increasingly worried about their apparently innocent questioning about his early background and family. On more than one occasion he was aware that Millie seemed bewildered by his evasive answers.

How long can I keep my identity a secret? he thought. Little did he know his precarious existence would soon be threatened yet again!

Chapter 15

A Reluctant Hero, Again!

It was gym first lesson of the day and John entered the school yard with his satchel across his back and his P.E. kit in a canvas shopping bag.

Noone remarked on this unusual method of conveyance, for there was a war on and make do and mend were very much the slogans of the day. Any type of protection of school wear was allowed.

The obligatory game of soccer was in full swing in the playground and John, who was quite a useful player, quickly joined in. The students were kicking around a bald, oddly-shaped tennis ball. As John swung his leg to kick it, the sphere bounced at an awkward angle and, instead of being propelled near to the ground, shot up into the air onto the flat roof of the gym's changing rooms. "Up you go and get it, young 'un!" shouted one of the older boys, "and be quick about it."

John, blushing furiously at his error, quickly stowed his satchel and gym equipment in a quiet corner and commenced shinnying up a drainpipe leading from the roof of the changing room. Most of the boys began to drift towards the main building as he climbed, for assembly time was fast approaching. The few boys remaining were concentrating on John's efforts and no one noticed Cowper, shielded by two of his cronies, as he quickly removed John's P.E. shorts from his bag. Taking a penknife from his pocket he quickly cut out the centre of the shorts, converting them to a skirt, placed the remnant in his pocket, and returned the damaged item to the bag. By the time John had retrieved the ball and climbed down again, the evil threesome had departed and the assembly bell rang.

It was a very embarrassed John who left school that day, accompanied by a cacophony of catcalls and wolf whistles along with comments about attending practice with the girl's hockey teams. As luck would have it, at least it was Friday, which gave him the opportunity to visit Whittle's Emporium on Saturday and buy another pair of gym shorts out of his meagre resources.

I'm glad I kept those spare ration books now, he thought, at least I can use the clothing coupons!

Late Saturday afternoon found John approaching Whittle's Emporium, still turning over in his mind how the Cowper gang had managed to carry out their dastardly deed. He was certain that one of them was responsible for the destruction of his gym shorts because of the sly smiles, nudges, and winks between the quintet which had been observed by Freddie, Millie, and himself during Friday's lessons.

As John neared the store, he noticed something unusual. Also approaching the door, from the other direction, was Mr. George, flanked by two strangers who were walking very close to him. Mr. George was far from his usual ebullient self. He looked pale, with a sheen of sweat on his usual florid features. The group passed in front of John as he paused at the store's main entrance. One of the two strangers spoke to Mr. George.

"Come on now, Whittle," he heard the stranger say, "straight in as though everything's fine and keep going 'til you get to your private office."

John frowned as he heard the words. "I've heard that voice before," he muttered to himself, "and if I'm right, it wasn't in very good circumstances." He quickly followed the threesome into the store, walking as close to the group as he dared. Suddenly Mr. George swerved to avoid a knot of parents and children milling in the foyer and one of the strangers was slow to change direction. Just for a brief instant there was a small gap between Mr. George and his companion. John stifled a gasp as he caught sight of a glimpse of metal in the man's hand.

He's got a gun and he's sticking it in Mr. George's back! I know they're going to rob the store. I bet the safe's in the private office! thought John. Then, he realised where he had heard the voice before: it was Nobby, the spiv's lookout who had tried to rob him of his spare ration books.

Once again John was faced with a dilemma; if he were to raise the alarm, Nobby might panic and fire the revolver. Also he would draw attention to himself which could only result in police interrogation and stories in the local newspaper. He continued to follow the group at a discreet distance, his mind racing, as the trio made their way through the crowded store towards the private office at the rear of the building.

Then, salvation appeared in a most unlikely form. As he turned into the upstairs corridor leading to the offices, John noticed a small red metal box with a glass front situated about his shoulder-height on the wall. Above the box was a neatly printed notice: *Fire Alarm In case of fire break glass and evacuate the store immediately.*

Mr. George was fumbling with his keys as he attempted to open the locked door to his private office. Both crooks were concentrating on this action. John quickly observed that no one else was in the vicinity, so he raised his elbow and shattered the glass. As the strident notes of the fire alarm rang out, he shouted in his deepest voice as he backed away from the scene, "Get out, Nobby, we've been rumbled!"

Further along the corridor, Nobby and his compatriot froze for a brief instant at the noise and warning call before sprinting along the corridor. They rushed down the stairs and barged their way through the crowds in the foyer and out into the street. A quaking Mr. George was left in their wake.

There was pandemonium throughout the store as parents and children struggled to leave the building. John lost himself in the milling crowd in the store. Nobby and his accomplice had disappeared and he sincerely hoped that they had only been able to give him a fleeting glance as he had retreated down the stairs.

It was much later in the afternoon before John was able to complete his purchase. A frustrated fire brigade team had established there had been a false alarm that was, in the words of the Chief Fire Officer, ". . . caused by vandals determined to sabotage the war effort." The police inspector also left the store with a detailed description of the two criminals.

Chapter 16

A Sporting Deception

The afternoon of the school under thirteen's soccer trial dawned bright and clear. John joined the group of thirty hopefuls who had been selected from forms one and two. The selection had been made by the sports master on observing play during the past few weeks. John was both strong and sturdy with a good eye for the ball and was pleased to be selected at number nine (centre forward) in the blue team. Opposing was the red team, distinguished by wearing red armbands! In goal for the red team was the imposing figure of Donald Cowper, who was sporting a brand-new, mustard yellow jersey and the very best in soccer boots.

As it was early closing day in Shrimport, the Cowper butchery wasn't functioning for the afternoon. A much larger and louder edition of Donald prowled the touchline shouting encouragement to his son.

The teams were evenly matched and with time swiftly running out the score was locked at two goals each. Some players had been substituted, but John, the scorer of the first goal for the blues, had more than held his own place. With one minute remaining, John's team gained a corner and the wingman's kick was cleverly caught on the goal line by the over-confident Cowper. Not being content just to catch the ball above his head, Cowper brandished the object in triumph and, in doing so, became slightly unbalanced. John, noticing the goalie's unsteadiness, rushed straight at him and administered a fair shoulder charge. Cowper and ball were shunted over the line and into the back of the net.

"Foul!" shrieked the entangled Cowper as he sought desperately to free himself.

"No way," replied the games teacher, "that's as fair a shoulder charge as I have ever seen; well done, lad."

"Rubbish!" bellowed Cowper senior as he rushed to free his still-trapped son, "You call yourself a referee? You couldn't look after a tiddlywinks game."

To add insult to injury, the games teacher patted John on the shoulder at the same time exclaiming, "Good, lad! That'll take Cowper down a peg or two. He's good when he's not showing off."

Both the Cowpers treated John to bellicose stares as the final whistle sounded. John shrugged his shoulders and turned away to the changing rooms. *What's one more enemy?* he thought. *I don't think they can cause me any more trouble at the moment.*

Later in the week, the under thirteen's selection appeared on the sports notice board and John was pleased and excited to see his name included as centre forward. The pleasure was short-lived, however, for alongside the team sheet was a list of fixtures for the season. First to visit John's school were Milton Secondary School; the very one he should have been attending under his real name of Jimmy Atkins, along with his former classmates from his Junior School.

There's bound to be someone in the Milton team who knows me, thought John, how can I possibly play without being recognised? I don't want to cry off sick; it could cost me my place in the team.

The evening before the game provided unwelcome visitors for Shrimport, but lucky for John as several bombers made an appearance with a lightning raid on the town. Bombs fell on Elton, most in the unoccupied area, but near enough to the apartment to jolt John out of his reverie on how he could possibly attend the soccer game. He now had an answer to his problem!

The games master and John's team mates were startled by his appearance when he arrived at the sports field the following afternoon. He had purposefully missed school that morning so that he could perfect what he hoped would be a good disguise. He had placed wads of paper under his top lip and inside both cheeks. His face and forehead were disfigured by several pieces of sticking plaster and he had applied petroleum jelly to his hair, which both changed the style he normally adopted and made it appear much darker than normal.

"Good heavens!" exclaimed the startled games teacher on seeing John's appearance. "You have been in the wars. Are you sure you're fit to play?"

"I'm all right, sir," replied John, "one of those bombs that dropped last night blew out a window and I caught some flying glass as well as banging my head on the floor. None of the glass stuck in my face and I still managed a good night's sleep."

"Very well," said the games teacher, "but I'll be watching you very carefully to make sure that everything's all right."

John was correct about the visiting team, for two of his former classmates had made the Milton eleven. Apart from passing startled looks at his unusual appearance, they made no comment.

The game finished in a 4-2 win to Acres Hill. John scored two goals. He went home well-pleased with his disguise and overall performance.

Chapter 17

Cracks in the Deception

It was mid-November when Freddie and Millie approached John in a state of great excitement as he entered the classroom.

"Have you heard the good news?" squeaked the pair of them.

"What good news?" asked John totally puzzled.

"The Winter Fair is coming to Shrimport," they chimed.

"Blimey!" exclaimed John, "with all their bright lights they'll attract every German bomber that can fly."

"That's where you're totally wrong," was the knowing reply from Millie, "'cos it's all going to be indoors."

"There's no building big enough in Shrimport to hold a fun fair," snorted a now totally bewildered John.

"One of the boys in form 3B has been talking about it," said Freddie. "He was at his uncle's in Crabville last week and the fair was there. It's all inside a big tent made of very thick canvas with special double flaps at the entrances and exits. This stops any light from getting out. I can't wait for it to come this weekend."

"Same here!" exclaimed an equally enthusiastic Millie, "the three of us can go after your evening paper round on Saturday. I'm going to raid my money box."

"So am I," retorted Freddie."

John was both excited and pleased for this break in his routine of school, homework, jobs, and the occasional soccer game.

Saturday evening was cold and clear. The threesome hurried to the site of the fun fair on Shrimport's main playing fields. Their informant had been correct, for there stood the largest tent they had ever seen. Once inside, they stood and stared, for flanking the structure were various sideshows where you could shoot small darts from air rifles at targets. At other stalls people were throwing floppy mops at cans, rolling pennies down chutes to win multiples of pence, and a coconut shy.

Occupying the central areas of the marquee were a children's roundabout, some swing boats and, at the far end, an adult ride known as the cock and hens. This roundabout was so called for the various carved birds people could ride on. In the centre of the ride was a huge steam organ complete with pipes and a multiplicity of carved wooden figures, garishly painted, who banged drums or clashed cymbals in time to the music.

John had thought long and hard as to how much he could afford to splash out from his hard-earned cash and had decided to spend one shilling. He had carefully counted out the twelve copper pennies, determined to make them last as long as possible.

The trio made their way to the adult roundabout and gladly parted with three pence each for a heady whirl on the noisy contraption. Next, it was the swing boats with John and Freddie taking turns to occupy one of the two-seaters with a squealing Millie; determined to gain maximum height for their money. Both Freddie and Millie had arrived with half-a-crown each. They began to spend the remainder from their thirty pennies with abandon, throwing at the cans, shooting at the targets, and rolling pennies down the chutes. John, now down to his last sixpence, was more cautious and stood back to enjoy the antics of his two friends. Eventually they arrived at the coconut shy and stood watching as a steady stream of adults and children attempted to knock down one of the three coconuts each planted on top of a metal stave.

None of the three objects were actually coconuts and the furthest south they had ever been was the Isle of Wight! Each was the size and shape of a small rugby ball, brown in colour, and stuffed with sand. Their surfaces were covered in matted strands of very thin, brown string stuck on to resemble coconut fibre. The strings had also been drawn together at the top to create a ludicrous fringe. No-one had been successful in downing a coconut, which wasn't surprising seeing as they squatted on top of a metal spike, in a saucer-shaped depression, on top of their poles.

"Come on now, roll up, sixpence for five balls," bawled the highly confident stall owner, "knock one down and win five bob."

John gasped at the thought of winning such riches as the sixty pennies represented the best part of a week's wage from his paper round. Before he could move towards the stall's proprietor, Freddie stepped forward.

"I'm game!" he exclaimed.

The stall owner, noting Freddie's small stature, made a surprising gesture.

"Go on, young 'un, move to the inside marker."

Freddie's nose crinkled at this special favour, for he had been allowed to stand at the throwing point for girls and young children. He quickly took aim and let fly. Though small in stature he did not lack either power or accuracy and, after scoring two glancing blows which, weakened the grip of the spike on one coconut, he managed to dislodge another.

"Got it!" roared the crowd of onlookers, as John and Millie danced up and down with excitement. The wincing stall owner was forced to pay out the five shillings to a beaming Freddie.

Before the coconuts had been reset, John stepped forward and took aim. The first four balls proved unsuccessful, but a minor miracle took place when he threw the fifth. Completely missing the coconuts, the ball flew through the air and hit the metal back plate a resounding blow before ricocheting into the side of the one that had been weakened by Freddie's efforts. As if in slow motion, the disturbed coconut slowing toppled off its stand and hit the floor.

"Bingo!" yelled the crowd, and to cries of "Pay up, mate!" the visibly reluctant stall owner was forced to hand over another five shillings to John.

As they moved away with their winnings, the stall owner shouted after them, "I don't want to see you lucky beggars again." Secretly he was far from annoyed, as the shy had drawn a large crowd all eager to try their luck and he soon recovered his ten shillings!

Flushed both with success and money, the youngsters were determined to spend some of it on further rides and treats. They made sure to include Millie. Eventually the two boys decided on one more trip on the adult roundabout and Millie, this time refusing the offer to join them, stood back to enjoy the scene. As the boys whirled round, a young girl standing next to Millie suddenly screamed and went deathly pale.

Millie turned to offer assistance. "What's up? Are you all right?" asked Millie.

"No!" replied the girl, still shaking, "I've just seen a ghost on the roundabout!"

"A ghost, what do you mean?" questioned Millie.

"There's a lad on that roundabout who's dead!" exclaimed the still-shocked girl. "That one there: Jimmy Atkins," she squeaked, pointing at John as he whirled by.

"How come?" asked a now-inquisitive Millie.

"I lived in the next street to him in Milton. Some months ago a bomb blew down his house and there was a big fire. Both he and his grandma were killed. It was all so bad that they never found anything of them. Now he's on that roundabout." At this point the girl started to sob.

"Come on now," soothed Millie, putting her arm around the sobbing child. "That's not Jimmy Atkins, it's John Adams from Elton. I should know. He works for me dad and we go to the same school."

These words of consolation seemed to calm the girl down. Shortly afterwards, she moved forward to be with her friends as they disembarked from the ride.

Millie quickly joined the two boys as they hurried homeward rather later than intended. Her mind was still in turmoil as she entered the side door of the grocery store and made her way upstairs.

"I'm going to get to the bottom of this mystery," she muttered as she climbed the stairs. "The more I learn about John Adams the more confusing it gets. It's about time he introduced us to his mum and showed us where he lives." She was still talking to herself as her parents glanced up at her appearance in the lounge.

"You're late," was her mother's greeting. Her father looked up from his newspaper and frowned disapprovingly.

"I'm sorry, but both John and Freddie won money on the coconut shy and we stayed on longer while they spent some of it," was Millie's quick response. "They saw me to the door, though."

"All right, I'll thank the pair when I see them," replied her mother, "now it's supper and bed for you."

Millie quickly disappeared into the kitchen, her mind still racing with ideas about discovering the truth about her friend.

Chapter 18

A Not Very Merry Christmas

The end of the autumn term at Acres Hill was approaching fast and John's determination to succeed was given its first real test. He had been lucky in his choice of friends, for both Millie and Freddie were very bright, as befitted scholarship children, and had helped John with his homework when he was struggling.

It was the first week in December when the class examinations took place and John faced up to the challenge of answering question papers, writing précis, and essays with his usual pluck. During the tests, the Cowper gang engaged in a series of dirty tricks, taking it in turn to distract the eagle-eyed teacher who was invigilating, in order to pass crib sheets to each other. They also took every opportunity to quickly scan their neighbour's answers.

John gritted his teeth as he observed their unfair performances, wishing that he could undermine their wrongdoings but unable to do so as he had to concentrate on his own work. It seemed the cheating group would complete the examinations unchallenged. The last of the tests was on history and John emerged from the classroom feeling relieved it was all over. He was somewhat perplexed when a grinning Freddie beckoned him over.

"What have you got to laugh about?" asked John, "that history paper was tough and I thought it was one of your weaker subjects?"

"It's nothing to do with my efforts," chuckled Freddie, "it's what Cowper and his gang will have written on their exam paper that's funny."

"What have you done, Freddie?" questioned Millie, who had joined them and overhead the last remark.

"I saw them copying key dates on the backs of their rulers," went on Freddie.

"You mean the ones they pass to each other when the teacher's back is turned?" chorused John and Millie.

"Yeah, that's right, but I borrowed their rulers when they went to the lavatories and managed to add a few noughts to some numbers and completely changed others. The history teacher will be surprised to read that Julius Caesar came to Britain around 550 BC, not 55 BC, and that the Romans came back again around 410 AD, not 41 AD. That'll teach Cowper to trip me up when I'm carrying a tray of puddings."

The following week turned out to be both exciting and troubling. First of all, what had been largely a European war since September 1939 had now developed into World War II. On December 7, 1941 the Japanese air force bombed Pearl Harbour in the Hawaiian Islands, sinking a large portion of the American Pacific Fleet. The USA was now in the war and pledged to help in the European struggle as well as in the far east.

"Shrimport's going to get really busy now," chirped Fred one morning, "those Yanks will soon be arriving by the boatload; I saw it in the last war. There'll be that much men, arms, and equipment on this island that it'll slip lower in the water!"

John chuckled at this last remark but, despite the historic events taking place, his mind was largely dwelling on what his exam papers would reveal. He was not to be disappointed, though, for his efforts had resulted in tenth position with Millie fifth and Freddie third. Their history teacher was particularly scathing with the Cowper bunch, failing all of them and commenting on their possible collusion and cheating.

To John's consternation, each pupil was given a sealed envelope addressed to their parents containing a tear-off slip to be signed by a parent or guardian and returned to school in the New Year.

"I'll have to get used to forging an adult signature and keeping a copy of it so it will look the same in future," he muttered.

The deception was getting harder and took a turn for the worse that weekend. John had just finished his grocery deliveries when he was confronted by Millie and her dad. "Me dad's got something to say to you," there was a mischievous glint in Millie's eyes, "it involves Christmas Day."

"Me, the missus, and young Millie here would like you and your mum to join us for Christmas dinner. We know just what it's like to be separated from family members at times like this. You've been such a willing worker these past few months as well as being a good friend to Millie. Anyway, we've swopped a few surplus groceries with Cowper, the butcher, and he's letting us have a goose from his farm. That, along with a tinned Christmas pudding from South Africa, will make a great meal. Come on, lad, what do you say?"

John was both blushing and confused by this unexpected turn of events and felt his eyes stinging with tears at this good-natured offer. He shook his head to regain his composure and then made his decision. No way could he jeopardise his independence by revealing his secret to the Martin family, even though it meant sacrificing such a lovely meal and the good company that went with it.

"It's really very kind of you and your family, Mr. Martin," he eventually managed to blurt out. "As you know, me mum's health only permits her to work part-time, but she has made a good friend at the factory. This lady lives just outside Shrimport and her husband is also away in the army. She has invited the pair of us to stay with her from Christmas Eve to Boxing Day, so, unfortunately, we won't be able to accept your very kind offer."

"Oh, what a shame!" exclaimed Mrs. Martin, "it would have been so nice to have a little gathering; ah well, it can't be helped."

Millie glared at John, her eyes blazing; once more he had explained away his mother. It was only with a considerable effort that she prevented herself from questioning him further about his Christmas arrangements as he made his farewells and left the store.

Millie was doubly determined to confront John and the elusive Mrs. Adams at the first opportunity. "I'm going to find out exactly where he lives and watch the comings and goings from that home as much as I can," muttered Millie to herself.

Fortunately for John, the pressures on Millie to help in the store, especially in the run-up to Christmas, sharply reduced any spare time she had to play detective.

Chapter 19

Cowper's Comeuppance!

It was a relieved John who returned to school in January, for he had spent a totally miserably present-free Christmas Day eating spam and chips for his dinner instead of roast goose with all the trimmings. At least he was back into a familiar routine again, which seemed to make time go quicker.

The academic successes of Freddie, Millie, and John had not gone unnoticed by the Cowper gang, who had suffered embarrassing chastisement by their parents following the history exam debacle. The group quickly returned to their bullying manner around the three scholarship children. John and Freddie ensured that they stayed together as much as possible outside the classroom, for isolation meant the possibility of fighting against overwhelming odds, especially in an era when teachers remained unaware of those being bullied!

The twice-weekly gym lessons became severe trials for John and Freddie as the Cowper gang missed no opportunity to kick, trip, punch, or push them around in any physical activity. Also, on the soccer field illegal tackles and shoulder charges became the norm. To make matters worse, Cowper, whose posturings as goalkeeper had exasperated the games teacher for too long, had been dropped from the under-thirteen's soccer team to be replaced by the lively and more agile Freddie.

Matters came to a head between John and Cowper well into the winter term but, strange as it seemed, not in or around the school premises. For two Saturdays running, John's bike had suffered punctures, which meant long wearying pushes to complete his orders and late finishes on his delivery rounds. Both Mr. Martin and Fred possessed tins of puncture repair outfits, so the inner tubes were soon mended.

"That first puncture looked like sheer bad luck," commented Mr. Martin as he helped John repair the damage, "but I can't explain how you came to get two holes in the side wall of the tyre for your second mishap. The roads must have some funny-looking objects lying in wait!"

"It's a mystery to me," a bemused John replied, "I'm as careful as I can be, for I don't like having to push this heavy bike around."

As he worked to repair the puncture, his mind went over the route he took and the point where the punctures seemed to occur. "I'm sure that it's more than a coincidence that both flat tyres developed near Cowper's butchers," he muttered to himself, "next Saturday, beware!"

The following weekend his delivery round proved un-eventful until he parked his delivery cycle near to Cowper's butchers. He carefully lifted off a box of groceries to carry up an alleyway and into the long, back garden of a house whose owner, who suffered from delusions of grandeur, insisted on back-door deliveries. As he turned to walk down the alleyway, he noticed out of the corner of his eye young Cowper and one of his cronies loitering in the butchery yard.

"I'll have to watch my back today," he muttered to himself as he carried his burden into the alleyway. This time, instead of taking the receptacle to the designated house, he placed the groceries on the cobbles and waited. Within seconds he heard footsteps as someone crossed the road; next he heard the chink of metal on metal and, at this point, he charged around the corner.

His suspicions had proved correct, for Cowper was bent over the delivery bicycle in the act of plunging a two-pronged fork into one of the tyres. So intent was Donald on his dastardly deed that he failed to notice John's swift approach. The warning shout from his partner-in-crime across the road came far too late for Cowper to react to his assailant's untimely approach. Despite Donald's larger physique, he was no match for John who was well and truly running on raw adrenaline. With one arm around his opponent's neck, he administered a half-nelson wrestling hold and used his free hand to pummel the choking youth across the face.

Cowper's crony still stood in the butchery yard as though paralysed, but his warning shout had attracted the attention of Mr. Cowper, who came running out of the meat preparation room at the rear of his shop. Initially he paused in shock at the scene that met his eyes, for across the road was his son, the light of his life, being half-choked and repeatedly thumped by an enraged youngster. To make matters even worse, it was the same boy who had charged his son into the goal net some time previously.

With a roar of rage he broke out of his reverie, sprinted across the road, and separated the combatants. "You little thug, I'll have the law on you for this, laying into an innocent child!" bawled an enraged Mr. Cowper.

"He's no innocent. The nasty tricks he plays on me and my friends, his gang are nothing but bullies!" shouted the still pumped-up John. "Look what he's just done to my tyre with that fork he was carrying!"

Unfortunately for John, the fork had somehow disappeared. Cowper's friend had followed the butcher across the road and now stood meekly to one side with his feet carefully covering the weapon.

"I thought his delivery bike was going to fall over and came across the road to steady it while he took his box of groceries around the corner," blurted a still-shocked but fast-recovering Cowper, "and this is what you get for doing somebody a good turn. Clip him, Dad!"

Mr. Cowper was sorely tempted to follow his son's advice, but refrained. Instead, he uttered a threat, "I'm going to have a word with Amos Martin about the kind of lad he's employing to deliver his groceries. A young miscreant who goes around thumping the innocent who are trying to help."

John was tempted to reply at this point but, seeing there were no other witnesses to Donald's dirty trick, realised how futile it would be. He slowly backed away to his box of groceries on the cobbles and carried on with his delivery.

The Cowpers and crony made their way back to the butchery where Donald and his accomplice were regaled with biscuits and lemonade to assuage the shock of the encounter.

Not for the first time did John make a slow and exhausting journey back to the grocers. He then recounted his tale to Mr. Martin who, following Millie's description of the Cowper gang and their devious antics, assured him his job was safe and all three bent to the task of repairing the puncture.

Somehow John was of the opinion that he wouldn't be getting any more punctures near Cowper's butchers.

Chapter 20

Nobby's Back!

It was late in the evening and the end of the summer term was approaching fast. John and Freddie had been invited to the grocery store to have tea with Millie and her parents after the business had closed. Once the meal was over, Millie's parents settled down to check on the shop's accounts, leaving the threesome to play games of ludo and snakes and ladders. After several ding-dong battles, the children began to discuss their actions in the impending summer holidays.

"I vote we spend some time at the beach," chirped Millie, "we'll have plenty of fun there."

"Its going to be a bit crowded," replied Freddie, "most of the area is covered in barbed wire and tank and landing craft traps. There's only a little bit left open for all of us to play on."

"I've heard that local farmers are looking for help to get their crops in. I bet there's plenty of fun to be had there, as well as both helping the war effort and earning some extra pocket money at the same time," chipped in John, always on the lookout to supplement his meagre income. He needed extra money to replace the clothing and footwear he was fast growing out of.

"That's a great idea," enthused Millie, "I'll check with my dad. Some of his suppliers will probably know whose looking for help and how we can get there."

Eventually it was time to go home and John, reluctantly, made his way back to his lonely room. As usual, he made a cautious approach to the former car showroom in the gathering gloom. As he neared his hideaway, he was startled to hear voices.

"I told you the place was a gold mine, Charlie. I've scouted this area during the past week and I've only seen one young kid walking through! There's loads of lead and copper just waiting to be picked up," rang out a voice that stopped John dead in his tracks. He quickly crouched down behind a pile of rubble.

"You're dead right, Nobby," crowed an exultant Charlie. "We can stack it in piles fairly easily tonight. Tomorrow night we can chuck it on the lorry in double-quick time."

"Right then, Charlie, let's get stuck in," replied Nobby. "It's money for old rope when we weigh this lot in."

The thieving pair moved off in the opposite direction to John, who occasionally caught a glimpse of a partially shaded torchlight and heard the sound of hacksaws rasping on metal.

He moved soundlessly to the apartment and slipped inside. "How am I going to stop this lot?" he mused, "at least I've got until tomorrow to come up with some plan." He settled down for the night.

By the following evening he had narrowed down his options to three widely different actions. Firstly, to open the lorry's bonnet and steal the distributor cap so that the engine wouldn't start. The problem was how to find the bonnet catch; the amount of noise it would cause when raised; the location of the holding rod to keep the cover open and finally to find the distributor cap. The second option was to let the air out of all the tyres, which would cause noise and definitely attract the attention of the thieves. Even then, after all his efforts, the lorry could still be driven away although the ride would be very rough and noisy. Third, and best, would be to unscrew the petrol cap, push a long rag down the filler pipe, and set light to it. The results would be spectacular but extremely dangerous for him if his timing was wrong.

As darkness fell, John crouched in the rubble and he heard the low rumble of a carefully driven lorry which pulled up in a central position adjacent to the piles of lead and copper. Both Nobby and Charlie jumped down from the vehicle after switching off the engine. They quickly concentrated on heaving the piles of metal onto a cushion of sacks placed on the bed of the lorry to deaden noise.

John crept carefully up to the vehicle having taken the precaution of lighting one of his slow-burning strings so the flash of a striking match would not attract attention. Both thieves were concentrating on the job in hand and failed to notice John as he felt his way around the vehicle to locate the petrol filler cap. After what seemed an eternity, but was only a matter of a couple of minutes, John's hand located the extended pipe that connected the petrol tank to the filler cap. Carefully unscrewing the cap, he pushed a dark-coloured rag as far as it would go down the channel, ensuring that just enough was sticking out for him to light. Now came the most dangerous part of the operation. He carefully ran his lighted string across the edges of the rag. Once he was certain the material was gently smouldering, he retreated at a slow and steady pace for some distance before he crouched down behind some cover and peeped out to watch the proceedings.

At first nothing seemed to be happening and John began to wonder if his plan had failed. Nobby and Charlie, now puffing and panting with their efforts, had reached the pile of metal farthest from the lorry, which turned out to be lucky for their safety. At this point there was a tremendous flash and a huge bang as the lorry literally jumped several feet in the air and came down on the road like a flaming meteor.

John, Nobby, and Charlie, although some distance from the blast, were bowled over by its effect but luckily avoided any of the flying metal.

"Come on, Charlie!" shrieked Nobby, once he had gathered his wits. "Let's get out of here before the rescue squads arrive. They'll think an old bomb has gone off."

John, although his ears were still ringing, heard most of Nobby's command and was delighted to hear fast-receding footsteps as the pair ran from the scene. As he made his way to the apartment, he heard the fast-approaching sounds of the rescue squad.

"Blimey," remarked one of the rescuers, "this place has seen some darned funny happenings recently."

Chapter 21

Harvest Time

During the summer holidays John, Freddie, and Millie spent an enjoyable time picking peas at several farms, interspersed with visits to the beach. The last farm on their agenda was approached with mixed feelings, for it belonged to the Cowper family!

As the trio expected, Donald and his cronies joined the gang of pickers and it wasn't long before trouble reared its ugly head! True to form, the evil quintet managed to pull off one of their dirty tricks whilst causing a distraction.

"Yippee! Look what I've just found," called Donald from the middle of a row of peas. He held up a circular piece of metal that glinted dully in the sunlight.

"It looks like an old sovereign," called out one of his cronies, "you lucky beggar, I bet you've found a crock of gold."

There was a general move in Cowper's direction as the pickers jostled to view the object. Freddie was one of the first to see the metal item at close quarters.

"Gold sovereign, my Aunt Fanny," chortled Freddie as he inspected the battered disc, "it's a brass button off an old uniform!" he informed the watching crowd who roared with laughter. Strangely, it seemed, Cowper did not seem at all disappointed with the let down and laughed along with the rest.

In moving to view the object at close quarters, Freddie had left his work basket unattended and, whilst all eyes were on Donald's find, one of the gang craftily placed several heavy stones under the picked pea shells.

"Blimey! This farmer's growing bullets, not peas," grunted Freddie a little later as he dragged his overflowing basket to the weighing machine to record his picking. The more pounds picked, the more he earned.

The weigh man was an old hand at pea harvesting and his eyes narrowed when a perspiring Freddie managed to heave his basket onto the scales.

"I smell a rat with this one!" he exclaimed, "and a big, heavy one at that. Let's just see what we've got here."

He tipped the contents of the basket onto a nearby table and revealed the stones amongst the pea shells. Freddie's look of outright astonishment at the incriminating evidence was met by an icy stare from the weigh man.

"Nowt for this basket, you little rogue, and if it happens again you're on your bike," he growled.

"Cheat! Cheat!" chorused the Cowper gang who had ensured they were lurking nearby in order to view Freddie's discomfort.

John and Millie were both appalled at Freddie's treatment, knowing full well who was responsible for this embarrassment but unable to prove it.

"From now on we pick as a team," suggested Millie. "That way we can keep a lookout for each other and share our earnings at the same time."

This move served them well and they finished their stint without any further mishaps.

Some days later, John and Freddie were summoned to the grocery store where Millie had some news for them.

"Me dad says he knows where we can spend a couple of days picking potatoes. Are you two willing to have a go?"

Freddie nodded his head and John literally jumped at the chance to supplement his funds.

"See you at the bus stop tomorrow morning at the usual time," called Millie as the boys left the store. She was sorely tempted to follow John. She was, frustratedly, no nearer to solving the mysteries that seemed to surround him. Just as she was about to track John, her father called her from the store and, sighing with exasperation, she reluctantly abandoned her detective work for another time and went to do his bidding.

It was hard back-breaking work as they followed the tractor-pulled machine that turned up the potatoes and picked up and placed the grubby objects in baskets. All went well for the first few hours, but then disaster struck. Millie, who happened to be closest to the machinery, suddenly noticed the potato-turning machine was heading straight for a suspicious looking fin sticking out of the ground between the tractor tracks.

"That could be part of an unexploded bomb," gasped Millie. "Stop the tractor!" she screamed, waving her arms at the same time.

The tractor driver failed to notice Millie's frantic signals, nor could he hear her above the roar of his engine. He was far too busy concentrating on his turn at the end of the row.

Millie dashed forward to jump onto the rear of the tractor, realising only her physical presence could get the driver to halt his machine. As she reached the tractor's tailgate, she stumbled and fell into the path of the oncoming turning machine. It was only John's quick-wittedness and sheer athleticism that saved Millie from a dreadful fate. He sprinted forward and dragged her across the front of the deadly machine that was bearing down. He managed to pull Millie clear, but at a cost to himself. One of the machine's blades caught his trailing foot and cut it badly.

"Quick! Wrap his foot up tightly!" shouted the farmer through the uproar that broke out around the injured youngster. "I'll get my car and take him to hospital."

"Can we go with you?" chorused Millie and Freddie. "We're his best friends."

"Come on then, make it quick," said the farmer, "time's important and he'll need a tetanus shot as soon as possible to stop lockjaw. One of my farmhands got gored in his leg by a cow and was dead within days because he didn't have the injection."

Both children shuddered at the farmer's story as they ran to his nearby car.

"One of you will have to go and tell his parents what's happened. If there's any operation involved, one of them will have to sign for it."

"His dad's away in the army and his mum works shifts. I'll tell her when she comes home," declared Millie. She watched as a pale-looking John was carefully lifted into the car. As she did so, she muttered to herself, "This time I will find out all about the John Adams family!"

Chapter 22

Off the Hook

Millie grunted in exasperation as her repeated knocking on the outer door of the apartment brought no response. "Drat it! His mother must be at work," she muttered, "still I've got plenty of time. I'm not due home 'til late tea-time. Mum and Dad still think I'm spud picking. I'm going to meet this Mrs. Adams if it takes 'til supper time."

Meanwhile, at the hospital, a nurse carefully unwrapped the tight bandage around John's injured foot. He winced visibly as she did so.

"There, there now!" soothed the nurse, "I believe that you acted very bravely."

Just then a doctor entered the casualty station and stooped to examine John's foot.

"You're a lucky lad! Well, I'll re-phrase that. You're unlucky enough to have got your foot cut in the first instant. But, on the other hand, the wound isn't quite as bad as was expected. So, no surgery for you, young man. Nurse White here is first class with needle and thread so she'll do a good job on stitching you up. Then you'll be able to go home, which is a blessing. There's no spare beds here anyway what with war casualties along with our normal intake. This darned blackout is causing more injuries in road accidents than Hitler's bombs! I trust that there's someone at home to keep an eye on you?"

"Oh yes," gasped a relieved John. Now he had no need to disclose his lonely existence. "Mum's at the factory, but I'm sure they'll give her a bit of time off to look after me."

"Right, John," the doctor continued, "before I move on to my next patient I'm going to give you an anti-tetanus injection. Nurse here will then wash your foot in an anti-septic solution and stitch the cut. Then, as long as there's no swelling or infection in or around the wound you can come back in a couple of weeks and we'll take the stitches out. Best of luck."

John nodded gravely and looked forward with some trepidation to the next part of the procedure.

Later that afternoon, a thoroughly bored and listless Millie was astonished to recognise the figure that slowly hobbled into view.

"John Adams, just what on earth are you doing here?" gasped Millie. "We all thought that you'd be tucked up in a hospital bed for a few days. I'd camped out here so that I could let your mum know what had happened to you when she came home from the factory."

"Well, I've saved you from your boring wait," chuckled a relieved John, aware that his secret was still safe. "I'll be able to tell her myself now. You'll have to let your dad and Fred know I won't be able to work for them for a couple of weeks."

Millie was both confused and pleased; once again she had been prevented from meeting the elusive Mrs. Adams, but at the same time her close friend was back on his not-too-steady feet!

"See you soon," called John as he let himself into the apartment, leaving a frustrated Millie to make her way home.

Chapter 23

Convalescence

John winced with pain as he stepped out of bed the morning after his accident. For a brief second, he had forgotten about his foot injury but placing it on the floor quickly brought him back to reality.

"Oh no!" he muttered later that morning, "it's going to drive me nuts being cooped up in this place for the best part of two weeks. Not only that, I'm going to lose my wages for the next two weeks, so most of what I've earned pea and spud picking is going to disappear quickly and I've still got some school items to buy. Gran's savings are going to disappear quicker than I expected."

The day passed slowly with John becoming increasingly gloomy and despondent.

"Should I tell Fred and Mr. Martin about my true situation?" he mused as he washed up the dishes from his frugal meal, swishing a few pieces of toilet soap in the hot water in a vain attempt to create lather and disperse the grease.

He was suddenly startled out of his reverie by an urgent knocking on the outer door of the apartment. "Coming, coming!" he shouted as he painfully progressed down the stairs. "I'm a bit hampered at the moment. Who's there?"

"Your friends!" was the collective shouted response to his question.

A startled John opened the door to be greeted by Millie, Freddie, Mr. Martin, and Fred. He had little choice but to let them into the apartment and they slowly followed him up the stairs.

John had long prepared for receiving visitors and had purposefully retained a few items of clothing belonging to the original John Adam's mother, along with a pair of her shoes. Some of these items were purposefully on view along with a spare cup, plate, and cutlery on the draining board! All were observed by the eagle-eyed Millie who whilst being reasonably placated by the evidence of a woman's presence in the rooms couldn't resist passing comment on the missing person.

"We seem to have missed your mum again, I see. Is she related to the Scarlet Pimpernel by any chance?" was her biting question.

The rest of the party looked askance at Millie's outburst. Mr. Martin, frowning deeply at his daughter's unusual behaviour, quickly intervened.

"We've all come to celebrate with yesterday's hero."

John blushed at being addressed in this way.

"I only did what anyone would have done in the same situation," was his modest reply.

"Nonsense, lad, it was a very brave act and shouldn't go unrewarded," remarked Fred, "and seeing as you can't work for us for a little while we've brought some goodies both as a thank you and to tide you over. I've raided my sweet stock and brought you a jar bottom selection! That is it's a right mixture of the sweets that stick to the bottom of the jars and didn't get sold for coupons. They're still good, though."

His little speech at an end, Fred emptied the contents of a canvas carrier bag onto the table to reveal several paper bags filled with pieces of treacle toffee, caramel fudge, and other delights.

John gasped with delight at the multi-coloured display.

"Not only that," interjected Freddie Wong, "I'm taking over your paper round 'til you're fit again."

"Aye, and I've been practising riding the beast and will be delivering groceries for the next two Saturdays!" exclaimed Millie, "but don't hang about getting well, that delivery bike hates me."

A burst of laughter greeted this heartfelt plea from Millie, and Amos Martin, who had briefly left the room, returned with a large cardboard box which he placed on the floor.

"Me and the missus can't thank you enough for what you did for our Millie. It's bad enough having two lads in the army facing who-knows-what dangers without having the young 'un here getting into such bad trouble. Anyway, to show our appreciation we've put together some grocer goodies that you and your mum can enjoy. It's the least we can do."

This final act of kindness was too much for John, who was unable to hold back the tears.

"It's great to have friends like you," he sobbed. "I haven't got much close family, but all of you make up for that."

Mr. Martin assessed the over-charged situation and spoke quickly.

"Come on folks, it's time for us all to go and let this lad get some rest. The past twenty-four hours can't have been easy for him."

The others nodded in agreement and made their way towards the door.

"I'll be popping in with library books and some of my old comics," called Freddie as he left the room.

"By the way, our Millie got it all wrong, you know. The bomb fin she spotted was no such thing. Last year the farmer had pigs in that field and the so-called device was nothing more than a piece of metal from the roof of one of their shelters," was the closing remark from Mr. Martin as the party trooped from the apartment.

Chapter 24

Very Welcome Visitors

The spring of 1943 arrived, bringing with it some radical changes to the population of Shrimport.

An excited Freddie greeted John and Millie as they met up on the first day of the Easter break.

"Guess what?" he exclaimed, barely able to contain his excitement, "a convoy of ships has arrived in the harbour and they're unloading soldiers and all kinds of equipment."

"There's nothing new about that," quipped Millie, puzzled by Freddie's behaviour.

"They're Yanks," whooped Freddie, "and there's thousands and thousands of them. Hitler's lot are in for a right bashing once these guys join in."

John and Millie's interest perked up at this good news. Although rationing and blackouts were still with them, air raids

131

had practically ceased and the war overseas seemed to be taking a turn for the better.

"Come on, then, what're we waiting for? Let's go and greet them," chorused Millie and John.

The trio, along with other youngsters, quickly made their way to a viewing point near the harbour to watch the proceedings. Unknown to John, Nobby, and Charlie, past adversaries were standing in a group of adults just behind him.

A large convoy of army lorries came out of the dock gates each crammed with soldiers. As one of the vehicles passed the children, one of the soldiers suddenly held up a large open box and plunged his hand into it. "Here kids, catch this lot!" he shouted, tossing a quantity of multi-coloured packets into the crowd of children. There was wild confusion and a melee quickly developed. Eventually, order returned and each of the trio emerged from the throng clutching trophies.

"I've got some packets of chewing gum," whooped Freddie.

"I've got something funny for ladies called nylons!" a puzzled Millie exclaimed.

"Look at these," crowed John, holding aloft several small packets, "salted peanuts and cashews, whatever they are!"

As John's voice carried to the crowd of adults behind them, a puzzled frown crossed Nobby's face. "I've heard that kid's voice somewhere before and it wasn't to my advantage," he muttered to himself. "Charlie, we've got work to do," he whispered to his compatriot.

"Don't mention that four-letter-word to me; I come out in a rash," chuckled Charlie.

"Be serious, you idiot," snarled Nobby. "See that little group of kids in front of us?" he pointed to our trio, "We're going to follow that one with the packet of nuts."

"You're not thinking of pinching them off him, are you?" questioned Charlie, "They'll hardly bring us a fortune on the black market."

"It's now't to do with today's happenings," replied Nobby, "if I'm right, that kid has caused us trouble in the past and if so he's for it!"

"Let's take our goodies home and meet in the park after lunch," suggested Millie.

Both the boys voiced their agreement, fully aware of the envious glances they were attracting from some older boys who hadn't been strategically placed when the gifts were bestowed.

Millie was the first to arrive home and received a startling reaction when she dutifully handed the packet of nylon stockings to her mother. "Where did these come from, and what did you have to do to get them?" asked the tight-lipped mother.

"I didn't have to do anything to get them," stammered a surprised Millie, completely bewildered by the tone of her mother's questioning.

"There, there then Flo," soothed Mr. Martin, "you're upsetting the lass; both of you sit down and take deep breaths."

"A Yank soldier threw them off a lorry down near the docks. If you don't believe me ask John and Freddie, they were with me and both got some kinds of sweets and chewing gum and passed some to me," wailed Millie, totally upset at

133

incurring her mother's displeasure when she had presented her with a rare gift. "Here are the sweets and stuff," she emptied her pockets onto the table.

"The girl's telling the truth, Flo," interrupted Mr. Martin. "I've just heard that the Yanks are setting up camp on some of Cowper's fields just outside of town. It's going to be a little while before they actually come into Shrimport, but it will certainly perk the place up!"

Mrs. Martin's snort of derision and worried look in Millie's direction did little to comfort the teenager, who realised her mother had mixed feelings about so many young male strangers descending upon the town.

Chapter 25

Kidnapped

John was totally thrilled by the contents of the packets that he had battled for and had briefly sampled one of them once he had separated from his pals. For once his guard was down as he walked along, concentrating on reading the details on the packets rather than on any surrounding persons. As he turned into the ruins adjacent to his apartment, he failed to notice that he was being tailed.

As the gruesome twosome cautiously followed John towards the car showroom, Nobby suddenly swore under his breath then addressed Charlie.

"There! I've got it; that's the kid who kicked me on the shins when he was trying to sell ration books. It was his voice we heard at Whittle's Emporium. He's been a right load of trouble. Oh no! I don't believe it! The kid lives in the only standing property in the square. A penny to a pound he had something to do with our lorry catching fire and blowing up. I always said it was no accident."

"What're we going to do about him?" queried a nervous Charlie, acutely aware of his partner's volatility and quickly mounting rage.

"We're going to nab him and give him a good hiding; nobody puts one across me," grated Nobby. "I'll stake the place out while you go and get the car and park it near the building. If we're certain he's on his own up there, we'll grab him next time he comes out. There's a good chance his folks will be at work and he's on his own. It'll be a while before he's missed and by that time we'll have sorted him out."

Charlie shuddered at the thought of what his partner could possibly do, but quickly made his way to the parked vehicle.

Meanwhile, Nobby settled down to observe any comings and goings from the apartment. Within the hour, Charlie returned with the car and parked close to the outside door of the building.

"I bet he'll be meeting up with his pals this afternoon. There's no way a kid of his age is going to stay cooped up indoors on a nice afternoon like this. Get those Cowper's meat pies out of the car; we won't go hungry while we are waiting. Once we grab him we'll take him to the cellar of that empty warehouse where we've stored stuff in the past. It's only about half a mile away."

Just one hour later, Nobby was proved right as the apartment's outside door slowly swung open and John cautiously poked his head outside to ensure that the coast was

136

clear. The careful opening of the door and John's tentative emergence gave the crooks ample time to rush in and grab the youngster. Quickly throwing a sack over John's head, they hustled him into the car, Nobby firmly clamping the squirming figure whilst Charlie slipped into the driving seat. The engine started and the vehicle moved away at a sedate pace over the road's poor surface.

Within a matter of a few minutes, the journey was completed and the struggling John was dragged down the cellar steps of the warehouse and deposited in a dank, dark room. The door was slammed shut and locked behind him.

"Nobby, just what are you going to do with him?" enquired the increasingly nervous Charlie as they stood in the warehouse yard. He had a little wish to add the crime of kidnapping to his criminal list of minor offences.

"I've not totally decided yet," chortled the exultant Nobby, "but remember this: when we grabbed him he didn't have time to lock up. It should be dead easy to jemmy open the inside door and turn the place over. There's bound to be something in there worth flogging to recompense us for our efforts. Remember, this little sod's cost us a lot of money in the past. As for later, a drive into the country and a good duffing up will teach him to keep his nose out of things. A long walk home will give him plenty of time to rue his actions."

"So be it," replied Charlie, "but before we go and do his place over I want a pint of draught. That pie of Cowper's was saltier than the channel and I've got a throat like cardboard."

"Okay, I'll drink to that," retorted Nobby, "let's go to the Mucky Duck; it's only round the corner. We can leave the car here."

The evil pair then made their way out of the empty warehouse and strolled at a leisurely pace to the nearby Black Swan public house.

Chapter 26

The Rescuers

Freddie left for his meeting with his friends earlier than expected as he had been given a parcel of laundry to deliver to one of the Wong's customers. The delivery address was far from the park but, after dropping off the garments, Freddie realised that the shortest route to the park would take him past John's home.

"I know, seeing that I'm still going to be early, I'll call for John, that'll surprise him," mused Freddie as he walked along.

As he approached the edge of the ruined area adjacent to the showroom, Freddie bent to tie a shoelace that had worked loose. Just as he was about to straighten up, his eyes were drawn to the drama developing at John's home. Two men sprinted around the side of a parked car, grabbed the startled John, threw a sack over his head, and quickly bundled him into the vehicle. Before the motor drew away, the quick-witted Freddie quickly grabbed a piece of debris and wrote the car's number onto a flagstone.

The youngster sprinted across the bomb site at an angle, keeping the slowly moving vehicle in view as he dodged between the shattered walls. Luckily for Freddie, the car turned into a cobbled cul-de-sac with an empty warehouse at the end.

Freddie waited until the juddering vehicle disappeared into the warehouse yard before running down the street and pausing at the gateway. As he peered around the corner, he was in time to see a struggling John being manhandled into the building. As the party disappeared he slipped into the yard and secreted himself behind a pile of debris.

No sooner had he settled himself than the two men emerged from the building and he listened in astonishment to their conversation before they left for the pub.

Down below, John had also been party to the conversation as the thugs had failed to notice that the cellar grating in the corner of the yard had been covered by a thin layer of rotting cardboard, which whilst obscuring the metal bars, didn't stop conversation from filtering through.

"It's that Nobby again," John muttered to himself, "he's like a bad smell that won't go away. How am I going to get out of this lot?"

Groping around the cellar, John eventually located a piece of wood which he was able to push through the bars and let some light into his prison. To his dismay he noticed that the grating could only be opened from the outside, but his efforts with the stick had brought him more than a ray of light, for a familiar and most welcome voice called to him.

"John, it's Freddie here," called out his close friend, "there's no way I can open this grating or the cellar door without a crowbar and that'll take time. How are we going to stop them burgling your flat?"

"Here, take these keys," replied John, quickly looping the items on the end of the wood and pushing them up to Freddie through the grating.

"Get them to Millie; tell her to go to the flat and when they start messing with the door, shout as though she's my mum; that'll put them off."

"Millie's at the park. That's going to take time and they've only gone for a quick pint round the corner. How can we slow 'em down?" questioned Freddie.

"Let the air out of one of the tyres, they'll think they've got a puncture, and they need the car to carry away anything from my place."

"Great idea," enthused Freddie, "but how did you get into this mess in the first place?"

"It's a long story," called John, "I'll fill you in later; in the meantime, ring the police from that call box near the park and tell them the blokes who tried to rob Whittle's Emporium some time ago are in a car in the bombed area of Elton."

"Whew! What've you been playing at?" asked Freddie.

"Just do as I say!" screamed John.

"Okay, okay, keep your shirt on," answered Freddie, "I'm off."

Freddie quickly sprinted away from the imprisoned John and made for the park as fast as possible. After making the phone call, he quickly outlined events to the startled Millie as they hurried to the flat.

"Just my sodding luck!" exclaimed Nobby as the two crooks approached the car. "I've gone ages without a puncture then this happens. Quick, let's get the spare off the back and get the wheel changed."

With grunts, groans, and much bad language the two set about their task and, to the listening John, seemed to complete the wheel change in double-quick time.

"Right, jump in Charlie," grunted Nobby, "that's a job well done; now we can go and sort his place out."

The car left the warehouse yard, bumped slowly over the cobbles, and eventually pulled up outside the boarded show-room. Nobby pushed the outer door and Charlie followed him up the stairs. A jemmy was inserted into the crack between the inner door and its frame and Nobby began to insert pressure on it.

"Who's there? What do you think you're up to?" shrieked a woman's voice from inside the apartment as Millie gave her best impression of a scared person.

"Blimey! This isn't on!" exclaimed a startled Charlie, who was, as usual, the more nervous of the two. "Let's get the heck out of here."

Nobby swore loudly, but reluctantly retreated down the stairs after Charlie.

Freddie watched from his concealed position as the crooks emerged onto the street and chuckled with glee as the astonished criminals were confronted by two policemen who had just parked their bicycles.

"Well if it isn't my old mates Nobby and Charlie complete with one of the tools of your trade," was the sarcastic comment of the police sergeant as he confronted the two villains, "come on now, that's not a toothpick you're carrying," he continued dryly as he pointed to the jemmy. "You'd better come quietly, reinforcements are on their way."

The two thieves stood there meekly as they were handcuffed and then forced to sit in their car.

"Look at this, Sarge!" exclaimed the constable as he checked the vehicle's boot, "there's a pistol in here and they're not even in the army!"

The sergeant quickly checked that the premises hadn't been forcibly entered and turned to address the baffled couple as a police car came into view.

"I think you two gentlemen are going to be sewing mailbags for some time to come if our information is correct," the sergeant observed dryly.

Once the police had left the scene, Freddie emerged from his hiding place with a stout piece of metal capable of forcing open the warehouse cellar door.

After collecting Millie, they returned to the warehouse to free John.

"This has all been a rum do; now let's get to the bottom of it?" quizzed Millie with a peculiar glint in her eye!

"Old Whittle's bound to recognise them," chuckled Millie following John's explanation, "and they'll definitely finish up in the clink."

Arm-in-arm, the pals strolled off to the park, none the worse for their adventure.

Chapter 27

Spies and Saboteurs

Later that year, John returned from his morning newspaper round to see great activity in the ruins surrounding the show-room. It was a pleasing sight, however, for several squads of American soldiers were dodging in and out of the ruined buildings and training for future house-to-house fighting on mainland Europe. The officers in charge had discovered the weakness in the damaged boards protecting the building and had moved inside to use the premises as temporary head-quarters while they assessed their troop's performance.

The manoeuvres continued for some weeks both during the day and some nights, but there was a sudden lull in late autumn in order to celebrate Thanksgiving Day (an acknowledgement of divine favours celebrated by the original colonisers of the USA.).

John still checked his approach to his accommodation, even more carefully since his kidnapping, and was surprised to see movement in the ruins, outlined by the moonlight, on the night of the Thanksgiving feast. He crouched down in the shadows and watched a figure carry two bulky containers into the debris and carefully conceal them. Making a mental note of the packages' positions, he followed the person leaving the ruins.

John suspected that he was trailing a thief or black marketeer who had concealed his ill-gotten gains and was surprised to see his quarry enter a tall, partially-damaged building, with only the top floor habitable, a short distance from his cache. As he watched, curtains swished shut in the top floor apartment.

"What's he up to?" muttered John, as he returned to the ruins to inspect the suspicious items. To his shock and horror, his torch beam revealed two mines complete with set time fuses.

These will probably explode when the soldiers are practising tomorrow, he thought. The military will think the soldiers have triggered two unexploded bombs from way back. At least I can leave warning notices on them.

The following morning there was uproar and consternation amongst the soldiers as they made the discovery. Mine detectors were brought in to make a careful sweep of the area both that day and any others whilst training took place.

John called a meeting with Millie and Freddie and outlined the events he had recently been involved in.

"Why didn't you go straight to the officers?" enquired Freddie.

"If I'd done that, the spy would have known that some-body was on to him. He probably thought his booby traps were discovered by accident," John replied. "What we've got to do between us is try and keep an eye on that building where he's living. He's not moved on, so there must be some other scheme he's working on. He'll always be on the lookout for any loitering adults, but us kids are like wallpaper—always around but mostly unnoticed!!

"I bet it's to do with the harbour," chipped in Millie. "From that height he can easily spot any comings and goings. If he's got a radio he'll be able to send messages to the French ports telling those E-boat commanders of any soft targets leaving Shrimport."

Both boys nodded solemnly at this statement for, like most of their generation, they had become immersed in the war's happenings and avidly devoured any information about their army's progress. Visits to see the plethora of war films at the local cinema had also fired their already-fertile imaginations.

"I heard one of those Yank officers saying that practised landings on our beaches from the sea were next on the list. Just imagine what would happen if the E-boats got in amongst those little boats. It would be a duck shoot," retorted John.

"Not if we can help it," chorused the other two.

The winter dragged on. In the spring, a flotilla of landing craft, along with their mother ships, anchored in Shrimport harbour. Within days, the American troops began their practise on the landing craft, initially in small groups, then in increasingly larger numbers.

"He's going to strike soon," prophesied John as the trio gathered for one of their regular pow-wows.

"Is it time to tell the police about him?" queried Millie. "At least it will stop any damage."

"If they go in now they'll just nab him, but if we time it right, we might bag more spies," was Freddie's thoughtful reply.

"He's been here some time now without raising suspicion, so that might make him over-confident, which could be his downfall. There must be some other contact equipped with a radio," said John.

"How do you work that out?" asked Millie.

"Well, if he was transmitting regularly from that building, our espionage agents would soon get a fix on it," answered John.

"Wow! How do you know all that?" remarked an impressed Millie.

"You'll be surprised what I've heard those American officers talking about. There's a gap in the floorboards under the bath and I've picked up all kinds of information. An intelligence officer was with them one day after the mine scare and they were talking about radio transmission. It appears all our spy two would need was a bicycle with a basket on the front. The transmitter could be disguised as a cabbage and you could park up anywhere in the countryside and get off a message very quickly," replied John.

"What we've got to do is trail him and watch where he leaves a message for his contact. Once we've followed spy two and found out where he lives, we can tell the police and they can do the rest," quipped Freddie.

"I'd rather not involve the police just yet," mumbled John to the surprise of his friends. "I know it sounds mad, but I'll tell you why as soon as I can."

Millie gave John a strange look. "You've always been holding something back from us, haven't you?" she retorted.

"Leave it there for the moment," intervened Freddie, noting John's evident embarrassment. "What's the plan, then?"

"We'll watch for the contact and take it from there. I've a good idea how I can nobble spy one, but it's up to you and, especially, Millie to catch spy two," replied John with a twinkle in his eye.

"I don't like that look on your face," retorted Millie, "you're planning something evil, aren't you?"

"True," John replied. "I want you to follow spy two 'til you see a policeman then bump into your quarry and scream blue murder. The policeman will come running and you and Freddie can hold onto the poor sod while you accuse him of pinching your bum and other parts. The bobby'll be down on him like a ton of bricks."

"Oh! It's all right for me to get involved with the police, but not you. What about my reputation?" shouted a crimson-faced Millie.

"Calm down, calm down," the diplomatic Freddie intervened, "it's a great idea. Once he's in the station I can phone the police and tell them they're holding a spy. The game's up

149

for him once they examine his papers—especially the newspaper—and search his accommodation."

Millie eventually calmed down and agreed to do what was asked of her.

"Leave spy one to me," a grim-faced John interjected.

The following day, there was massive movement around the harbour. Hundreds of American troops boarded the mother ships that left the harbour towing the landing craft behind them bound for a trial beach landing.

As the build-up was taking place, spy one left his lair and made his way to a park bench where he sat for a few minutes reading a newspaper. After a few minutes, he left his seat and casually tossed the newspaper into a nearby rubbish bin before returning to his eyrie.

The trio watched the procedure from secure positions and split up to follow the conspirators. John to dog spy one, whilst the others tagged on behind spy two once he had retrieved the newspaper from the bin.

John waited outside the ruined building and, having double-checked to ensure only one person was inside, entered the apartment block and crept up to the landing below the spy's apartment. He then mounted the last flight of stairs and carefully tied a piece of string across the steps, securing it with a metal staple on the wall side which he knocked into the wooden panelling with a sock-covered shoe to deaden the noise. Retreating to the landing he lit a pile of dampened newspapers with a match and wafted the smoke upwards. The through-draft from the windowless floors aided his efforts.

Very soon, the smoke was dense enough for him to carry out his strategy.

"Fire! Fire!" he roared, "get out quick! The building's going up in flames."

Within seconds, the apartment door opened and spy one rushed into the smoke and down the stairs. A loud yell reverberated through the building as the unsuspecting agent tripped over the string. This was followed by a loud crash, a crack of breaking bones, and screams of agony. Then there was silence as the spy passed out in shock.

"Got you!" a triumphant John exclaimed," you deserved every bit of that."

John looked down on the motionless figure and pinned a notice to his chest.

THIS MAN IS A SPY. SEARCH HIM AND THE TOP FLOOR FLAT.

Quickly covering the smouldering newspapers with a wet blanket, John dashed down the stairs to the nearby phone box to call an ambulance.

A short time later, a relieved John, hiding nearby, saw an ambulance arrive. Eventually, paramedics pushed a bound stretcher containing the still-unconscious enemy agent into the back of the vehicle.

"We'll have to get the police in on this once we get this poor sod to hospital," remarked one of the ambulance men to his colleague. "One of our undercover agents must have sorted this one out good and proper!"

A triumphant John returned to the park where he was soon joined by an excited twosome.

151

"It worked like a dream," crowed Freddie, "the poor guy didn't stand a chance against Millie; Hollywood, eat your heart out!"

"Never get me involved like that again!" exclaimed Millie, wagging a finger at John and grinning at the same time. "I've never been so embarrassed in my life. At least the police agreed not to tell my parents about the incident. Mum would have had a blue fit."

"Well I reckon we saved a lot of lives today," remarked Freddie, "there doesn't seem to be much peace and quiet with John Adams as a friend!"

Chapter 28

Finale

D-Day, June 6,1944 came and went. Once the allied forces had safely established a bridgehead in Normandy, the town of Shrimport became relatively quiet—especially after the departure of the American soldiers.

The trio were now practically inseparable and had earned the nickname at school as The Three Musketeers. As the year passed, Fred's health deteriorated and John, but also Freddie, took on more of the responsibilities at the newsagent's.

As 1945 dawned, it became obvious Fred couldn't carry on with his business much longer. In late spring, John was amazed he was called into the back room one day and greeted by Fred and Mr. Tompkins, a local solicitor.

"Sit down, lad," ordered Fred, "Mr. Tompkins wants to say something to you."

"I've heard such a lot about you, young man. You have a very generous and appreciative employer who has named you as sole beneficiary in his will," was the clipped reply.

"What does all this mean?" asked a puzzled John.

"I've not long to live," was the blunt answer from Fred, "and when I've gone, everything of mine will be yours."

John shuddered at the news. Fred's news left John in tears. Someone who had been like a benevolent granddad was going to die.

Later that morning, John broke the news of Fred's decision to the Martins who, whilst comforting the upset youngster, didn't seem too surprised by Fred's reactions.

"There, there then, John," soothed Mrs. Martin, "he thinks the world of you, and so do we. Why, our Millie just can't stop talking about you, it's forever John this and John that!"

"Shut up, Mum," squawked Millie, who had just come in on the conversation. "Can't you see you're embarrassing both of us? We're just good friends, that's all."

"Tell that to the Marines," chuckled Mr. Martin. Then, in a mock fierce voice, he addressed John. "I've got my beady eye on you, young Adams; you'd better watch yourself around our Millie."

"I don't know what you're talking about," gasped a confused John, feeling the day's happenings were too much for him.

"There's still things we don't know about you, even after all this time," remarked Mrs. Martin. "We've never met this shy elusive mum of yours. When are we going to meet her?"

"It won't be long now," answered John with a wry smile.

John woke early, as usual, on the morning of May 8, 1945 and made his way to the newsagent's to mark up and deliver his newspapers. He was most surprised to be greeted by an ailing but exultant Fred who raised a glass of whisky to him as he entered he shop. "It's happened at last, lad. War in Europe's over and I'd saved some whisky to celebrate. Now you, young man, can really start living again." (He was unaware of the years of rationing and austerity that would stretch into the 1950s for a thread-bare and virtually bankrupt country).

"It's not been all bad for us; what you never had you never missed," replied the ever-optimistic John. "All right, toys and presents have been few and far between but look at the good friends I've made and the generosity you and the Martins have shown me."

The day passed in an atmosphere of euphoria, culminating in a street bonfire where the long-stored fireworks provided a fitting climax.

During the last week of summer break, John called his two friends to a special meeting in the park.

"Sit down you two," said John in a serious voice. "I've got quite a bit of explaining to do."

He proceeded to tell them of the deception he had carried out for practically four years.

"I knew it! I knew it!" exclaimed Millie, wiping tears from her cheeks. "It's ages since I discovered there was no Mrs. Adams, but I thought it better for you to come clean about it. Remember, I was on my own in your flat when those crooks were trying to break in and curiosity got the better of me. I had a good root around and it soon became obvious there was only one person living there."

After this revelation, John pressed on.

"Now I want to show you where I used to live and how lucky I was to escape the bombing."

The trio left the park and made their way into Milton on their way to the bomb-damaged Smedley Street.

As they were approaching the area, a conversation was taking place at the end of Smedley Street between a policeman and a soldier leaning on a walking stick.

"I was still fighting in France when the British forces were evacuated from Dunkirk," explained the soldier. "My platoon didn't get out of southern France 'til nearly two months later. The military was still in chaos when we got back to the U.K. After de-briefing, we were put on a train to northern Scotland for re-training and re-equipping. By the time I was able to write to my family, the bombs had already fallen here and that was it," he slowly wiped the tears from his face. "Then it was north Africa, Italy, Normandy, and eventually a parachute drop on the Rhine."

"Is that where you were wounded?" asked the sympathetic bobby.

"Aye, I suppose it was a mix of good and bad luck. The bad being shot through the foot as I was floating down. The good being it wasn't too bad an injury and the war was over before it had completely healed."

John outlined his plans to the others as they approached Smedley Street.

"So you see, I wanted to tell you now as I'll soon be sixteen and out of the reach of the authorities, also I'll probably not be going back to school. I can't afford to carry on with my studies as I've no savings left; instead I'll probably be working full-time at the newsagent's."

"That's a shame," replied a visibly upset Millie, "you've proved to be a more than capable scholar and I'm sure the school would be expecting you to stay on 'til you're eighteen and then go to university."

"Ah well," sighed John, "dreams are dr—just a minute! Who's that?" he exclaimed as he caught sight of the soldier at the end of the street. "No! It can't be? Yes! It's Dad! Dad!" he shouted as he ran to the soldier, leaving his stunned friends in his wake.

The soldier turned to face the source of the noise.

"Jimmy, it's a miracle!" choked Sergeant Major Tom Atkins as he crushed the youngster to his chest. "Everybody said you were dead."

"Well they were wrong, weren't they?" came John's (Jimmy's) defiant response.

"Come and meet my closest friends and I'll explain everything."

Needless to say, there was a joyous reunion at the apartment a short time later with friends and extended family present.

John/Jimmy did go back to school as a demobbed father was able to manage the newsagents and provide the financial support the youngster needed.

Yes, you've guessed! The Phoenix was reduced to ashes once more as Jimmy Atkins took his rightful place in society. His joy was completed when Millie became Mrs. Atkins with a beaming Freddie as best man at their wedding!